THE HEALER

Linda McClung

THE HEALER
Copyright ©2022 by Linda McClung

ISBN: 978-1-63945-369-6 - Paperback
       978-1-63945-370-2 - ePub

All rights reserved. No part of this publication may be reproduced, distributed, or transmitted in any form or by any means, including photocopying, recording, or other electronic or mechanical methods, without the prior written permission of the publisher or author, except in the case of brief quotations embodied in critical reviews and certain other noncommercial uses permitted by copyright law.

Although every precaution has been taken to verify the accuracy of the information contained herein, the author and publisher assume no responsibility for any errors or omissions. No liability is assumed for damages that may result from the use of information contained within.

Printed in the United States of America

Writers' Branding
1800-608-6550
www.writersbranding.com
orders@writersbranding.com

Contents

Definition of Terms vii
Prologue ix

PART I
Slavery
Ten Years Later

Chapter 1 3
Chapter 2 7
Chapter 3 13
Chapter 4 23
Chapter 5 27
Chapter 6 35
Three Years Later 39

PART II
Freedom

Chapter 7 47
Chapter 8 53
Chapter 9 63
Chapter 10 69
Chapter 11 73
Chapter 12 77
Chapter 13 87
Chapter 14 91

PART III
Persecution

Chapter 15 101
Epilogue 111
Endnotes 113

For Noah John and Liam Joshua, my two strong young men.

Even strong young men and women need a Redeemer.

And to the glory of Jesus of Nazareth,
the Redeemer, Teacher, Healer, Son, Jehovah.

Definition of Terms

In scripture, the names given to Jesus of Nazareth reflect his character and mission. I give a simple explanation for those not familiar with the many names used for Jesus the Christ.

Yahweh – the proper name of God found in Genesis 2:2. Jewish tradition calls Him YHWH, a word so holy that it could not be pronounced. As vowels came into use, it was changed to a pronounceable name with vowels. It means Lord and master

Yehoshua – was the earliest name of Jesus and was shortened in later biblical texts to Yeshua

Jesus – a translation from the use of Jesu which came about with more modern English

Messiah – throughout the Old Testament, the Messiah is anticipated, described, and hoped for by the Jews. He would be the promised deliverer of the Jewish nation and to the world

Christ – a New Testament adaptation of the word "Messiah" prophesied in the Old Testament who was to come

Master – seems to come from the disciples who called him several things, including Teacher, Rabbi, Lord, and Christ

King of the Jews – this was the sign placed on His cross at the crucifixion. It was put there by Pilate who wanted to shame Jesus, but was a final indication of who He is, King, and Christ

There are many names the Jesus used for himself: He called himself the Bread of Life, Lamb of God, Light of the World, Son of Man, Son of God. These each have an important part in understanding who He was and why He came. Other characters from scripture include the following:

James and Titus – named as half-brothers of Jesus who came to belief after his resurrection
John the Baptist – one who was prophesied to come as a messenger to prepare the people for their Messiah
John the Disciple – one of the fishermen who called himself "one who was loved." He was given the responsibility for Mary after the crucifixion
Luke – a Gentile physician who wrote the gospel of Luke and Acts
Mary – the mother of Jesus and tradition tells us that she assisted Luke and the apostle Matthew in writing the gospel story
Simon Peter – one of the disciples who became their leader in the days following the Feast of Pentecost

Prologue

The sun rose over the peaceful valley as always. Chickens pecked lazily in the courtyard while blackbirds cawed at them trying to get to the grain. Noah had risen early to prepare for the day, but first he must gather firewood, go to the market for the feast tonight, and clean his sleeping area. His family and the priests from their temple were gathering for the evening celebration.

Noah knew he would be required to recite the long scripture passage he had learned at the temple school. He still did not understand the meaning of the verses, but he had not been able to find anyone to explain them. The priest mumbled something about mesiah, but he wasn't sure how he felt about the concept of Jehovah God, even though he had accompanied his father to the synagogue and watched him pray daily at home. He liked being a Jewish boy, but that was as far as he was willing to go with religious training. He would do what was expected of him, but to believe with his whole heart like his father did not seem necessary.

Just to be sure he was ready, he began no practice the verse he had memorized from the prophet Isiah.

> The Spirit of the Sovereign Lord is on me,
>   because the Lord has anointed me
>   to proclaim good news to the poor.
> He has sent me to bind up the brokenhearted,
>   to proclaim freedom for the captives
>   and release from darkness for the
>   prisoners.[1]

"Noah, come quickly," his sister interrupted.

"What is it?" He replied.

It was just like Miriam to have an emergency right when he had big plans for the evening feast. She was two years older than he and had already become a helper to his mother. She was a good sister, but sometimes she was so annoying. She seemed to know just when to ask for help when it was the most inconvenient.

"Mother wants us to set up for the evening meal and the guests will be here in one hour!" She yelled.

"Can't you do that? I need to get ready. I am the guest of honor, you know," Noah retorted.

"No," she replied. "I need to prepare too, so Mother said we must work together." "Okay, I'm coming."

Noah did not have time for this, but he knew his mother would be disappointed if he did not help. Miriam knew where everything was stored, and she was already setting out the utensils and linen cloths. Noah hurried through the task, making sure everything was set out to Miriam's approval. He finished as quickly as possible so he could hurry back to his room to prepare himself for the celebration of his bar mitzvah. This special day would mark the end of his childhood. It was a day of celebration for all Jewish boys and their families, and he was proud to be the guest of honor.

All his friends at temple school were planning their special day. They were busy memorizing holy scriptures and considering what gifts they wanted. He did not want to ask his parents for any gifts as he knew they were poorer than his friends. His father was a shepherd and as such, they barely had enough food for their family. Going to the temple school was a great sacrifice for his parents, but they were adamant that he must learn to read.

The Healer

Even though they were poor, his family was generally happy. They worshiped together on the Sabbath at the synagogue where Noah and his brother accompanied their papa to the men's inner court, while Miriam and their younger sister stayed with Sarah in the women's court. There he had learned the prayers of the Jews to Jehovah and could recite them from memory.

As the oldest son, he had the responsibility of helping his mother watch his younger brother and sister. His older sister helped his mother in the house, since they were too poor for servants. Today, everyone was helping prepare for the celebration to honor Noah's bar mitzvah.

All Jewish boys celebrated the time they could be called "men" by their families. The boys' family would no longer be held responsible for their wrongdoings; instead, they alone would be held accountable to Jehovah. If they were wealthy, the families would shower the young men with gifts, but Noah did not expect many gifts from his family. Instead, they would celebrate with their friends and enjoy the best they had available.

Sometimes the boys at temple school laughed and made fun of him because of his ragged clothes and worn sandals. He had to learn early in life this was going to happen. He tried not to get into fights with them, but when he did, one or two of the boys went running home with bloody noses. Eventually they learned to leave him alone as he grew taller and stronger.

The house filled up as the guests began to arrive right on time. It was a small house, so guests spilled out into the courtyard to eat, drink, laugh, and discuss the political issues of the day.

Noah was nervous and stayed in the corner trying to be inconspicuous. The priest from his temple approached him, started slapping him on the back, talking about what a great joy it was to be a Jewish man in Jerusalem. His papa said that the men of the temple could have so much more influence over the Roman government if they just stuck together and demanded change. Noah did not expect the men to resolve anything today so, he watched as they continued with their discussions. His papa nodded in agreement as they rambled on.

Noah had not given much thought to the political issues facing his people. They had been ruled by the Romans since before he was born, but his family lived in peace and stayed out of their way. He decided to stay quiet during this exchange because he did not feel that he had anything to contribute.

He spent his days studying at the temple, but during his days free from study, he and his friend Rocco liked to roam the streets of Bethany, playing catch, riding donkeys left on the streets, or chasing other boys. It was something to fill their days, and Bethany didn't have much for a young boy to do. When they had the courage, they would walk to Jerusalem where they could grab some food from vendors, hide it under their cloaks, and run for their favorite hiding place to enjoy the snack. Rocco was good at this, so Noah just followed his lead. Getting caught by the Roman soldiers was a scary thought but so far, they had been lucky with their forays into town.

Dinner was full of laughter and good food. Noah's mother, Sarah, had prepared all his favorite dishes. They started with a pot of soup seasoned with legumes, wheat, and barley followed by bread made with wheat, barley, beans, lentils, millet, and emmer dipped in local olive oil. Best of all was Noah's favorite, the fig cakes flavored with local honey from their neighbor. She had put out the best linens, and everyone seemed satisfied and happy.

As the time drew near for him to stand and recite his scripture passage, he longed for someone to stand with him and take away his fear. He still wondered about the meaning, but they were words he had memorized, and they were all that was required today. With a big breath, he stood, steadied himself, and began to speak:

> *The Spirit of the Sovereign Lord is on me,*
>   *because the Lord has anointed me*
>   *to proclaim good news to the poor.*
> *He has sent me to bind up the brokenhearted,*
>   *to proclaim freedom for the captives*
>   *and release from darkness for the prisoners,*
>   *to proclaim the year of the Lord's favor*
>   *and the day of vengeance of our God,*

> *to comfort all who mourn,*
> *and provide for those who grieve in Zion—*
> *to bestow on them a crown of beauty*
> > *instead of ashes,*
> *the oil of joy*
> > *instead of mourning,*
> *and a garment of praise*
> > *instead of a spirit of despair.*
> *They will be called oaks of righteousness,*
> *a planting of the Lord*
> *for the display of his splendor.* ²

He didn't stumble over a single word. His family stood and congratulated him with cheers, hugs, and kisses, and words of congratulations. Today he would assume more responsibility for his family. They could finally start treating him like a man.

His father approached him with a very solemn face, and Noah's heart dropped. What did he miss? More than anything, he did not want to disappoint his papa. Noah just hoped he hadn't done something wrong on this day of celebration. He had chosen the scriptures carefully with the priest, and they had agreed that he would use this one.

"I have an announcement," his papa began solemnly. "This is a very important day in the life of my son, so tonight, my son will join me in the fields with the flock. He is ready to join us to care for the sheep."

Noah stood staring at his father. For years he had begged his father to let him go to the fields and help with the sheep, but always it had been, "No, not yet." Tonight, would be his first time to join the men at their task of minding the sheep. He felt like his heart would burst with joy. The only sorrow was that Rocco would not be there with him. His friend did not have a father, so he was free to run and play and sometimes even get into trouble. But Noah did not care about that. Rocco was wild, fun, and unafraid of anything. He liked Rocco and his free spirit, but his friend would understand because he was headed to the fields with his father. Nothing could be better!

When they arrived at the pasture where the sheep were quietly grazing, the other shepherds were already preparing for the night with a campfire going with food on sticks ready to eat. Noah looked around for other young boys but only saw a few teens who were already playing a game on the ground. Since he really didn't have a chore to perform, he just sat and watched.

After a while, Noah's eyes grew heavy with sleep. His father hardly noticed since he was busy with a roaming sheep. When he saw Noah asleep, he did not wake him, deciding instead to let him sleep for a while.

Sleep had just overtaken Noah when he was awakened by loud noises, singing, and flashing lights. He was startling into alertness, thinking it was a strange dream. Fear caused him to first search for his father. "Papa, where are you?" He cried. By now he was saw that he was not the only one afraid, with the strange noises and lights that surrounded the meadow.

"I'm here, son!" Replied his papa. "Come and see what is happening."

Noah, hearing the sounds, thought maybe it was another group of shepherds singing. But why would they be singing in the middle of the night? The night sky was as bright as day. There, hovering close by, were beings who looked like men, but were singing and not even touching the ground. What was it? He had heard of angels from the priests at the temple, but he had never seen such a sight. They were coming down very near to them singing:

Glory to God in the highest,

And on earth peace to men on whom his favor rests.[3]

What could they be talking about? He must still be dreaming. What kind of men sang and hung in the sky like that? Then one of the men came closer and spoke to them. The light bathed him in a heavenly glow so bright it was hard to look directly at them. All the men shrank back from the messengers and covered their faces.

The angel said, *"Don't be afraid. I'm here to announce a great and joyful event that is meant for everybody worldwide: A Savior has just been born in David's* town, a Savior who is Messiah and Master. This is what you're to look for: a baby wrapped in a blanket and lying in a manger."

Then there was a huge group of messengers singing like they were in the temple. Noah heard "Hallelujah" and "Glory," and then they just disappeared. Complete silence surrounded them with no indication that anything different had occurred in that place. With no warning, all the men began talking at once.

"Let's go!" One said.

"But what about the sheep?" Said another.

"We can leave them with the young men, so let's go!" Said their friend Zack. "We have to go to Bethlehem to see this thing that God has told us about."

Zeb turned to the men and said, "Don't you remember your holy scriptures? It tells us where the Messiah would be born."

> But you, O Bethlehem Ephrathah,
>   are only a small village among all the people of Judah.
> Yet a ruler of Israel
>   whose origins are in the distant past,
>   will come from you on my behalf. [4]

"Do you suppose this could be a child born to be our Messiah?" Zeb continued. "He did tell us to go to Bethlehem. That's David's city and not too far away."

"We have to go see this child that God has sent," Zack responded. "If he is the Messiah we have been looking for, it will change everything."

Noah was looking at his papa to see what he was going to do. To his amazement, Papa was putting his things in a sack and getting ready to leave. That would be so great if he could accompany the men and it would be something to tell Rocco later. Papa just turned to him with a nod and said, "Let's go."

Noah quickly put his sleeping blanket into his sack and turned to join the men. As they began their walk, questions began to swirl in his head. What was this all about? Why would messengers be talking to them? There was no logic for heavenly messengers to be talking to his papa and his friends. They were so poor, they had to mind sheep at night to make a living. None of them had gone to the temple for an education, and all were dirty ragged men of the lowest class. He knew he would also become one of them when he grew up. He had learned to read by the many sacrifices of his parents, but he still wasn't sure he would be anything other than a shepherd.

What would make a messenger from heaven come speak to them about a baby being born in Bethlehem? It was all very confusing to him, but the men were determined to find some answers.

"I tell you, friends," his father said, "this could be the One. God has promised us a Savior from the time of our father, Abraham, and if He has arrived in Bethlehem, I'm going." Noah thought he had never seen his father so excited.

"Maybe you are right, Zeb," replied Zack. "But what I don't understand is the baby. Why would God send a baby to be our Savior? He can't wear a crown and form an army to defeat the Romans. It means we will be under Roman rule for another twenty years while he grows up, so we are going to be no better off than we are now."

They were aware of the dangers and persecution from the Romans for almost a hundred years. Sometimes Jewish men simply disappeared, never to be found. Many Jews were pressed into service to levy heavy taxes on their fellow Jews. It was a dark time for their people, so the hope of a Messiah was often discussed.

Papa's shoulders relaxed as he turned to his friend, Zack. "I don't have all the answers to these questions. You know the holy scriptures don't say that He will lead an army. Maybe this baby will provide a way for us to know God in a better way. Or maybe He will not need to lead an army. Remember our forefathers did not have an army to defeat the Egyptians. They walked across the Red Sea on dry land and the Egyptian army drowned in the sea. Jehovah fought the battles for them. We are going to have to trust Jehovah just as they did."

The Healer

By this time, Noah was too tired to even think about his questions. His papa was moving determinedly onward, and no one even suggested a stop to rest so, Noah walked on as well.

"We are almost there," said Zack. "I see cattle and a cave ahead. Let's try there." He began to run toward the small group of people gathered ahead.

On a Sloping hill outside of town, Noah could see the stable Zack spoke about. It was a cave dug into the hillside, with cattle and some sheep wandering around outside. He hung back and watched because he was still feeling that flutter in his stomach that told him he should be afraid.

He watched his papa walk right up to the couple standing inside the cave.

"Good evening!" He yelled out. "We heard that a special baby has been born here, and we came to see for ourselves."

"Yes," replied the young man. "He is here. Come and see."

Noah watched as his father approached the feeding trough. There was the little baby, new and looking like a sleeping baby. He watched as his father crept toward the feeding trough, then kneel and place his face to the ground in worship. Were those tears in his eyes? Noah tried to see more and moved closer to see the tears and his father looking at that baby like he was seeing Jehovah Himself. His father stayed there for a long while, watching the baby with tears flowing down his tired face. The tears did not seem to be sad ones, but tears of pure joy.

The baby never made a sound as the other shepherds came, and like Zeb, they too knelt to worship. They stayed around the stable for a long time talking to the couple and inquiring about this baby. The young mother said her name was Mary and her husband, Joseph. She told them a story about seeing an angel several months before and being told that she would have a child. She even told them that she was not married at the time. Noah sensed that this story was getting personal. What could she be thinking? But Zeb and the others listened intently, showing no surprise or judgment. They watched as she gently took the sleeping baby and held him. She sang a lullaby to him while the shepherds stood and watched in awe. She explained that they were in Bethlehem to pay their taxes but would be returning to Nazareth when they could travel.

It was time to go, and even though they were tired, the shepherds were excited about telling their friends and family about this baby. Gone was any thought of sheep tonight. Only one thought remained. This was news for the whole world, and they would be the first ones to tell it!

"Fellas, I think this is the One we've been waiting for. We must go tell people. I want to tell my family!" Zeb said excitedly.

"I want to tell my brother, "Another said.

"We have to tell the whole town. We've been waiting for this for centuries."

Noah headed to his home and fell into a deep sleep. When he awoke, he was all alone. The men still had not returned, but he could hear voices buzzing on the streets. It would be many years before he realized he should have paid more attention to the events of this night.

PART I

Slavery Ten Years Later

Chapter 1

Noah and Rocco had big plans for the day. It was market day in Jerusalem, which meant there would be great opportunities for two young men who needed to eat. Food and trinkets would be in abundance, and Rocco had perfected the ability to snatch and run. He was so fast he had never been caught as he nicked some fruit or stuck a trinket under his shirt. Rocco was the best! He had a keen eye and quick hands, so the soldiers did not have a chance to catch him.

Noah did not feel so confident. He knew he was slower and more likely to get caught, so he usually let Rocco do the deeds. Maybe today he would go ahead and get some desperately needed food for dinner. He had been practicing his skills when his father was not present. Times had been difficult in Judea with no rain for months. Now that he was twenty-two, he could no longer spend his days playing but was expected to bring some income to the family. He had been unable to find work, but the market provided good opportunities to take what one needed. He knew it was wrong to steal the food, but he was desperate to help his hungry family.

Noah had grown into a handsome young man. He was still slender as a reed by the river. He was trying to grow a full beard, like Rocco, but it seemed to grow slowly. His hair was the color of the sand of the Judean desert and hung in waves to his shoulders. Everyone said he looked like his father, but he did not see any resemblance. He loved his father but was trying to be stronger and faster and show his father that he could provide for the family. He still helped with the sheep at night but spent his free time with Rocco.

Rocco was his best friend. He lived with his mother and younger brothers and sisters. His father had disappeared when he was young, and Noah wasn't sure he was still living. Rocco supported his family by stealing food and any jobs he could find. He never committed crimes that hurt people, but he did steal from vendors, gardens, and any food left unsupervised.

Rocco was waiting for him outside in the courtyard. They took a few minutes to plan their strategy. Noah told Rocco his idea that he should be the one to grab the food first because his family needed food for the evening meal. He would take the chance even though his heart hammered in his chest.

"No, Noah!" Rocco pleaded. "You know I'm better at this than you are. I'll make sure your family eats tonight."

"I'll do it." Noah could be stubborn. "It's my responsibility."

"Okay, friend, but wait for my signal," Rocco replied.

Rocco was still reluctant but agreed to this plan, so they set off toward the market. Noah kept alert for any sign of soldiers around. There was one lazily standing next to the meat market making sure no one stole those valuable items.

Noah and Rocco quietly passed the meat stand and began searching for other unwatched food available. They spotted a stand with cabbages and other greens while the owner was busy chatting with his neighbor. Noah decided this was the one. The time had come to show Rocco that he could do this. He looked at Rocco and gave a quick nod. It was time. He looked around and did not see anyone watching, but when he reached for the cabbage, his hand was suddenly caught in a vise-like grip.

"What do you think you are doing?" A soldier stood over him holding his arm by one muscled hand. He must have been seven feet tall. His eyes were dark, his black beard covered his brooding face, and his broad chest strained the tunic.

Where did this guy come from? Noah had no chance to speak before he was jerked by the collar and marched down toward the magistrate. He turned his head from side to side looking for Rocco. All he saw was the back of Rocco's tunic while he clutched a cabbage as he raced down the path, weaving in and out among the vendors. No soldier followed him.

Noah had no idea what to expect from the magistrate. He tried to imagine what he could say to get himself out of this mess. His father was out watching sheep, his mother was home caring for his brother and sister. He was supposed to be the responsible one and bring home dinner for all of them. There was no hope of that now. He was filled with dread as he considered the possibilities before him. He had no money to offer to pay his debt and no one to speak on his behalf.

The magistrate sat on a big seat, in a purple robe, waiting for wrongdoers like Noah. Was there anything Noah could say that would help him? He knew he was guilty of theft, so what excuse could he make? There were too many soldiers around to make an escape possible.

Fear covered him like a blanket. His mouth was dry, his knees trembled making it was impossible to stand still. He looked down at the red clay stones at his feet and thought this must be the worst day of his life.

The big soldier holding onto him began speaking to the magistrate. "I caught this guy stealing food. I've seen him in the market before this, and I knew what he was up to. There is another one just like him, and I will get him too. I say you should send this one away. Get rid of some trash."

"What do you have to say for yourself?" The magistrate said as he turned to face Noah.

Noah was too scared to form words. Nothing would penetrate the cotton in his mouth. What if he asked them to find his father? That probably would take days, and by the time they did, Noah could be long gone. Maybe the truth would be helpful, but he could not form the words.

"So, you have no excuse. Well, then I sentence you to five years of labor. Take him away."

The magistrate calmly turned to face the next offender, and just like that, Noah was led away to face the unknown.

Chapter 2

It felt like days that he had been tied up in the back of the bumpy oxcart. His hands and feet were never loosened, nor had the guards given him water or an opportunity to relieve himself. He had not eaten anything all day, and now the sun was low with no indication they were near their destination. As the sun began to set, he saw they had traveled south from Jerusalem but he had no idea how far they had traveled.

The road was rutted, and the cart kicked up dust that covered everything, clogging his throat and burning his eyes. They traveled downhill for much of the journey and if he could have looked, he would have seen the beautiful blue haze on the mountains to his left which should have told him where he was.

The day might have been beautiful if he had been able to turn his head to the sky. From where he lay, he could only see the rough boards of the cart and hear the rumble of the wheels as they turned on the hard-packed dusty road.

During those long hours, Noah relived the peaceful hours with his father in the sheep meadow, how sweet the grass smelled, how the sunshine enveloped the men as the sun rose over the Judean mountains, and the long talks with his papa during the walks to and from the meadow. He thought of his sweet mother when the winds blew her scarf into pillows of blue around her face and how she sang hymns of praise to Jehovah while she washed their clothes and ground the grain for their bread. He even longed for his sister and remembered her eagerness to learn alongside him when he came home from temple school. Now he wished he had been more patient with her and his little brother and sister. He couldn't conceive of a life without his family.

Several more hours passed in this way. Noah was hungry, exhausted, and the bindings were hurting his arms and legs. The guards laughed and drank cool water but did not offer Noah anything to drink. He felt like a dog caught stealing scraps for dinner thrown into the back of the cart.

Finally, they slowed to a stop. The guards jumped down and yanked Noah to his feet, but he stumbled and started to fall. The guards grabbed his shirt and hauled him up, ignoring his difficulty standing.

"Okay, young man, we have arrived. Come meet your new master." They laughed.

"My feet…" Noah whispered.

"Hold still!" The guard growled as he stooped to untie Noah's feet. "But don't try anything. You may as well get used to the idea that this is your new home."

He had wondered what kind of "home" he would face. Would it be a small one like his home with Mama and Papa, or would he face a life of hard labor with some rich merchant? He looked around his surroundings and saw many fields of grain. Servants hurried about performing a variety of tasks, caring for oxen and donkeys, working the fields of grain, and washing clothes in a tub. He could see a well where women were carrying jars of water in and out of a big house.

This must be the master's house, he thought. It was a large complex with room for the animal below and apartments above for the master and his family. There was a large courtyard surrounded by a stone fence. Fig and almond trees were growing along the edges and orchards of carob and jujube trees were growing on the hillside.

Noah had just looked around quickly when a man about his father's age came striding forward. He was not a tall man, but he walked with authority. He had a dark beard covering his scowling face. His robes were scarlet, and his head covering was encrusted with jewels. There was no mistaking this was a man of wealth and influence.

"Good, you are finally here. Bring that young sapling in and I'll take it from here," he barked.

With determined strides, the guards dragged Noah forward and tossed him into a shed which looked like it was made to house oxen. The floor was covered with dung, there was no window, and the roof was going to leak when it rained. The small door slammed shut, and he could hear the master latching it, so there would be no chance of escape.

"I'll take care of you in the morning!" He heard the master growl. Then all became quiet.

Noah was alone and completely helpless-a prisoner in a dungeon. He was hungry, thirsty, and tired. Even if he could escape, he had no idea where he was. His parents must be worried about him by now. He had no way to contact them to let them know he was alive. How could he endure this for five years? He needed someone to help, but so far there had been no one.

He did not know anything about grain. He thought of all the time he had wasted with Rocco when he could have been learning a trade. All he knew was how to care for sheep. Maybe the master would let him take care of the sheep. Did they even have sheep on this farm? He thought of trying to escape, but that possibility was quickly fading.

Noah looked around and found an area that was relatively clear of dung and lay down. He had no hope of getting food tonight. He could hear his stomach growling but tried to ignore it and get some sleep. His last thought before sleep was of the priest in the temple talking about a promised Messiah who would set them free. *Free!* How that word rang in his heart. Could he be free one day? His ancestors had been slaves for seventy years and Jehovah had rescued them and sent them home. Maybe he still had a chance!

A loud crash woke Noah from his sleep. "Wake up, kid, time to get to work." His guard this time was a young man not much older than himself with ragged garments, and a haunted look on his dirty face.

He scrambled to his feet, followed his guard out the door, toward the grain fields.

"I don't know anything about grain," he murmured. But his guard ignored him and did not stop to ask questions, nor did he even offer food to break the fast. He brought Noah to the threshing stone and showed him how to push the large wooden handle to turn the stone to separate the grain from the chaff.

"You just have to turn the wheel and the wind will do the rest," he said. Was that an ugly grin on his face?

Noah put his hand on the wheel and gave it a push. Nothing happened. He pushed harder. Still nothing. The next time he gave it all he had. Nothing. Then a guard arrived with a whip made of strips of leather with metal attached. He was taller than Papa, who everyone said was a tall man. He had muscles that strained his tunic, hair down to his shoulders, and hands the size of horses' hooves.

"Get moving!" The guard snarled.

'I can't get..." Noah pushed with all his might but was unable to get the handle to move more than a hand's breadth. He was not a weak man, but this was an impossible order. *What can I do?* He thought.
"I said to move it!" The guard yelled.

"I'm trying." Noah pushed with all his might. The large man did not reply but raised the whip toward Noah, and before he had a chance to think about it, he felt a hot blaze of pain across his back that brought him to his knees.

"I said to move it!" He registered the man's shout but could not get his legs to move or the handle to turn.

Again, the white-hot blaze seared his back, and Noah moved his legs enough to attempt to stand. What could he do to escape this torture? The thresher was made for something or someone much stronger than he. There was no chance of moving this thing.

As he knelt there trying to pull himself to his feet, he felt the pain again, and this time when he fell to the ground, his world going black. He did not feel the fourth and fifth strikes of the whip.

Chapter 3

The world was a swirl of flames, hot embers, and pain. The only thing that kept the blazes away was the black curtain that would sweep over him. He could escape into a world where he saw sheep grazing in green pastures and fathers gathered to laugh at someone's funny stories. Days and nights melted together in pain that roared from his head to his feet. How long he lay there, Noah was unaware. But when he did rise above the darkness, the pain of his back would not let him escape. His mouth was parched, his body ached, and it hurt to move even a little. He heard someone walking about in the room but had no way to know where he was or who was caring for him.

"Son, good, you're awake. Here, drink some water."

The voice he heard was low and soothing as he moved about the room. He was an older man, close to his father's age. His clothes were ragged but clean, and his hands were calloused but gentle. He smelled of jasmine and eucalyptus as he moved in closer and sat on a stool nearby.

"Go slowly. You've been very sick. Take your time," the man said.

Noah tried again with some success and lay back to take a better look at this man who was so kind.

"Who are you?" Noah croaked

The man had dark skin, with silver hair and beard. He had hands so large they could span the rump of a sheep, but gently held Noah's head to drink. His deep-set brown eyes sparkled with laughter even at this serious moment. He stooped down to be at eye level with Noah and near to his cot.

"My name is William. I've been here since I was your age. I've served my time and decided to stay since I had nowhere to go. The master isn't too bad. I know he would not approve of what happened to you. He was away on business, so I try to look out for the young ones, but I was busy that day. And boy, you do need someone to watch for you. I'm just glad someone thought to come get me before you were hurt even more." William smiled at him and lifted his head to give him more water.

"How long have I been here?" Noah asked.

"Three days now. I was not sure you were going to live. You got a fever and your back looks like a plowed field. You've been talking out of your head for days now. I've been trying to get you to drink water for me, but you couldn't even hear me."

Noah drank all he could, but he was already feeling the darkness settle over him. He lay back and closed his eyes while the pain in his back circled until he gave in to the darkness.

The next time he woke, he could smell something delicious. How long had it been since he had eaten? He wasn't sure but thought that it had been breakfast that last day at home. How long had that been? Four, five days.

He tried to sit up, but the pain of his back roared through his body. His hunger won out over the pain, and he looked about for the source of the aroma. The room was small and sparsely furnished with a cot on which he lay, a stool, and a small table for a candlestick. It had a plank floor which indicated to him that someone gave special attention to this home. The breeze through the open door cooled his feverish body.

"Here, let me help you."

William was immediately at his side gently lifting him to a sitting position. He handed Noah a bowl that smelled of meat and broth. He took a few bites, and it tasted as good as it smelled. He finished the food and handed William the bowl.

"You can have more later," William reassured him. "I need to change the bandages on your back. The first time will be painful, so take this and drink to help ease the pain." He handed Noah a small portion of a bitter-tasting liquid.

He did as William instructed, and it did feel better very soon. But the dressings stuck to the open wounds on his back and were painful to remove. William was gentle, wetting the dressings and moving slowly. He applied a terrible smelling poultice to the wounds, then some clean cloths, and by the time he finished, his wounds no longer throbbed.

When Noah awoke next, his pain had lessened, and he was able to sleep soundly.

It must have been several hours later he heard voices in the distance. He aroused from his sleep but did not move. There was another person in the room. He had never heard William use the tone of voice he was using to the stranger. He heard William say firmly, "Enoch, you have got to be more careful with that whip. You could have killed that young man out there. If this happens again, I'm going to have to let the master know about it, and he won't be too happy with you."

"You have got to make them listen and respect you. If you don't, they will just run away, and we will spend valuable time hunting for them!" Enoch growled. "A little beating never hurt a boy. It will turn him into a man."

"Still, it's my job to keep them healthy, and this young man won't be able to work for weeks now, if ever," William replied softly, with a hard edge to his voice. "He's a good one and did not deserve such treatment. You gave him more than a little beating. You nearly killed him."

Noah heard the door close and a chair creak as William settled in beside him. He again closed his eyes and drifted into sleep feeling grateful for someone like William to help him get through this. He knew that he could trust this man who would speak to that guard so boldly. Maybe he had found someone who could help him survive this ordeal.

The next morning, when he turned, he was surprised the pain in his back had eased, and he was able to stand by holding onto a chair. He was encouraged to realize his back felt much better. He felt his stomach rolling with hunger just as William came through the door with a tray of food.

"Hey, young fella. I see you're feeling better." He had a merry laugh as he set the tray for Noah to break his fast.

"Yes, it is better. What did you put on my back? I had no idea this would heal so quickly!" Noah exclaimed.

"Oh, this is an old remedy my wife used to fix up for all kinds of cuts and scrapes. It comes in handy when Enoch gets too aggressive with that whip."

"Sounds like he has done this before," Noah stated in disbelief.

"Oh, yes," William replied. "When someone new comes in, I always have to watch out for them. Enoch likes to establish his authority early on. Now, back to bed with you."

Each day Noah increased his time out of bed walking about in the small room trying to get his strength back. He endured the painful dressing changes knowing that they were necessary. Between walks, he ate heartily, slept soundly, and tried to let his body recover.

After six more days of resting, Noah was ready to go outside. He longed to see the sky, feel the wind on his face, and listen to the birds or insects looking for food.

"When do you think I will be able to go outside?" Noah asked William as they finished the care of his back. "I feel like getting some fresh air."

"Soon as you eat this," as he set the tray beside him. "I'll set you up with some tools that need cleaning. That way you can be busy when Enoch comes by."

That sounded like a great idea to Noah who had always been handy with tools. Before the sun had moved over the roof, he bathed and changed into a clean tunic that William provided. His legs felt stronger and moving no longer caused his back to ache. The stool was right outside in the courtyard with a basket of broken tools next to it.

Noah sat and breathed in the warm, clean air of his beloved Israel. He could see the mountains in the distance and was able to orient himself to his location. The cool breezes bathed his face while Noah thought about all that had happened to him. The only person who had been friendly was William, who was so much like his papa. He would make sure to stay close to him in the future.

Noah dove into the basket with excitement because he had never seen so many tools at one time. Papa would have been excited to see this, he mused. Then he began to think of his papa and the times they had walked in the pastures and talked of many things, but mostly his papa talked about the holy scriptures. What was it that he always said about a Messiah? He was always looking for signs of His coming. And then that night at the manger his father kept saying, "This is the One."

Noah hoped he was correct in that, because Israel surely needed a mighty king and warrior like David of old. Someone who would fight their battle against Rome and shake off their oppressors. Then maybe Noah could go free. The magistrate had said five years. Such a long time to survive in this place of torture. Ah, freedom! How he longed for that when he had never given it a thought before his capture. Someday, he would find a way to go free.

Then he thought of Enoch and how his hated whip was still being used on the innocent slaves. Something had to be done to stop that monster. He didn't know if he could stop him, but he vowed to try if he ever got the chance. While he had no plan of escape, he could try to make life easier for himself and the other slaves.

It was still dark outside the next morning when he was awakened by loud banging and shouting.

"Lazy, lazy one, get up! It's to the fields today for you!"

He knew that his time away from the fields would probably end soon, but if he had to return to the hated thresher, he was doomed. He hastily pulled on his tunic, grabbed his sandals and a drink of water, and left his bed. His guard today was someone new—a young man not much older than himself who wore the rags of a slave. He walked briskly out of the hut and toward the fields, bypassing the hated thresher.

"Come, you are to work here. Gather the grain stalks and bring them into piles. Try to keep up with the cutters, don't fall behind," he spoke with such authority it was difficult to see him as one so young.

The work was not difficult, but he was always behind. When he tried to speed up, his back began to ache with the bending and stooping required. The sweat ran down his back and arms, causing his open wounds to burn again. At times, the sweat ran red from the bloody wounds. His muscles ached from the unaccustomed exertion. Being in bed for a couple of weeks had left him weak. He seemed to be getting slower and slower as the day wore on.

Around midday when the sun was straight overhead, he heard someone shout, "Halt!" Noah stopped and looked around and saw a servant arriving with a basket of bread. Everyone walked toward the shade, so he joined them as they sat in an orderly fashion while the bread was passed around. No one remarked on his presence. They simply ate in silence, drank from a common jar, then slowly began to trickle back to their workplaces.

Work resumed as it had all morning. Noah's arms ached with the unfamiliar activity, so by the time he heard, "Halt!" He was exhausted and hungry. Again, the workers walked to the shade trees and sat to wait for their portion of food. There was bread and a few figs and cheese, which disappeared quickly.

He began to understand the importance of getting his food before it ran out. Then he noticed that the servants were wandering off to their huts, and not returning to the fields so, Noah walked back to William's hut. At least the slaves were able to stop working at a decent hour allowing them time for rest. His wounds needed attention and he really had no other home.

William greeted him warmly. "So how did it go?"

"It was all right. I did not have to work the thresher today," Noah replied.

"Ha-ha, I didn't think so. They usually put the oxen on that thing." He chuckled.

"What?" Noah exclaimed. "You mean they knew I couldn't move that thing?"

"Of course not. They just wanted to see what you would do. They like to put the new slaves on that thing. I'm sorry this happened to you. If I had been here, I would have stopped them. I'll make sure it never happens again." William moved closer to him and put his big arm on Noah's tired, aching shoulders. "You'll be all right, you'll see. Now we need to see about your hut, a more permanent place to call your own."

Noah followed William with trepidation. He liked living with William and had secretly hoped he could stay. He had no idea what to expect as they wove around various huts until they arrived at the very end where there was a rundown pile of sticks and mud fashioned together into a hut with a roof that surely leaked when it rained. William marched in through the opening where a young man of about twenty years sat on a bed of straw. His face was dark and brooding, and his clothes were ragged and dirty, he was thin to the point of skeletal. He didn't look up as he and William entered.

"Daniel, meet Noah. He will be sharing your hut. You need to clean this place, its filthy."

Noah raised his hand in greeting but received no greeting from Daniel. With that introduction, William turned leaving Noah standing in the hut smelling of animal dung, rotting straw, and human waste. He looked for a place to make his bed but could find no area decent. He could see he would have to clean the hut in order to stay here. It looked like no one had cleaned the hut in a long time, but Noah's home had always been immaculate. He would find a way to make this small space more acceptable, even to his own mother.

"Help me clean this place. It's not fit to live in," Noah turned and spoke directly to Daniel. But the man remained silent in the corner and seemed unaware that anyone had spoken.

Well, he thought to himself, *that will have to change. I don't plan to live in this filth.*

He knew there was at least one person who would help him. He raced back to William's hut and begged for a rake and some fresh straw and blankets. William nodded in understanding. "Sure, I'll be over shortly and help get that place in order."

William helped him rake out the dirty straw and haul in clean bedding. They even changed out Daniels' dirty linens and put clean straw and bedding for him. William gave Noah a table and several stools. It began to look more like humans lived there. He thought he could further improve the hut but living with this shell of a man was going to be difficult. Daniel stayed in the corner and never met his eyes. He had never had trouble making friends before, but he had never met anyone who acted like Daniel.

When he had a clean pallet and fresh straw on the floor, there was still time to find out about this man he would be living with. He went back to William with his questions.

"So, what is Daniel's story?"

William shook his head and sat silently for so long, Noah thought he would not answer. Then he said, "None of us have been able to get him to talk. He came here when he was just a little boy for stealing or something like that. Most of us can't even remember why he came. He's never had a loving family, and he has made no friends here. I tried to be his friend, but nothing worked. If you try to reach him, I wish you good luck."

Noah left intrigued by someone who had never enjoyed a family and determined to try reaching this sad and lonely person. He knew how important his family had been to him and could not imagine his life without them.

The days ahead were all the same. Early rising before dawn, backbreaking work until mid-morning, a meal, more work all afternoon until sundown, when another meal was served. His back healed slowly, leaving tracks of scars that would be with him forever.

The Healer

Noah was free to do as he wished each evening, and most days, he wandered back to William's hut to sit and talk until bedtime. Each day he would invite Daniel to come along but was always ignored. William loved to talk about the leaders of the Israelites from long ago. He would often talk of the prophet Daniel's faithfulness while a captive, and Elijah, Isaiah, and often of Abraham. His favorite was King David who loved Jehovah God but had made some terrible mistakes. He loved to quote some of the songs from David:

> The Lord is my shepherd, I lack nothing.
> He makes me lie down in green pastures,
> > he leads me beside quiet waters,
> > he refreshes my soul.
> He guides me along the right paths
> > for his name's sake.
> Even though I walk
> > through the darkest valley,
> I will fear no evil,
> > for you are with me.
> > your rod and your staff,
> > they comfort me. 5

One day William began to talk about Joseph, a young man who was the beloved son of Jacob and great-grandson of Father Abraham. Joseph had been unjustly sold by his brothers into slavery in Egypt where he had been a sent to serve in Potiphar's house. He was a slave to the Pharaoh for over twenty years. He said Joseph had worked his way up to second in command to Pharaoh himself and eventually helped save the entire Israelite nation.

"How did he do that?" Noah wondered aloud. He had heard of Joseph from the old priests in the temple, but now the story had more meaning. Slavery in Egypt was something he could identify with!

"Joseph used the gifts that Jehovah gave him. He had been able to interpret dreams since he was a boy, and now, he was able to interpret dreams for his captors. He made himself valuable to the Pharaoh by interpreting his dreams. The Pharaoh listened and gave Joseph responsibility for the entire nation during a famine. Many people tried to bring him down, including

Potiphar's wife, but Joseph remained faithful to Jehovah even though he was a prisoner."

Noah went home that night with many questions in his mind. How could he make himself valuable to the master? What gifts did he have that could be used here on this farm? He had to find a way to improve his conditions here. He would soon be twenty-three years old and no longer a boy. He had his whole life ahead of him. Would he spend it as a slave? Joseph had been only a boy of seventeen when he was sold, Noah reminded himself. He knew he was smart, but he had never been able to interpret dreams. There had to be something else he could do.

For the next several days, Noah could not get the thoughts of gifts out of his mind. He would sit alone at night and review his likes and dislikes, his preferences, his skills. What were his gifts? He liked people but lately his love for people had been challenged by those in charge of the slaves in this camp. His encounter with Enoch had made him afraid of all the guards. Daniel was withdrawn and hated everybody and would not speak to him. His coworkers often did not speak his language. Only William seemed to want to be his friend. Still, he would think about the stories he had heard about Joseph and how his dreams had led to his opportunity to speak to the Pharaoh. Noah could not think of any gift that he could use to get the master's attention. He could read, but so far, he had no opportunity to read anything.

Chapter 4

One night, Noah began to ponder the idea that Jehovah God might be able to help him. His father believed that Jehovah answered prayers and was always praying about every aspect of his life. Noah tried to pray but did not know how to begin. In desperation, he decided to just talk to this God that the rabbi had told him about—the one who had parted the Red Sea for the Israelites and had fed them manna for forty years in the desert.

"Jehovah, if you are there, I need you right now. I need something or someone who will help me get through this. I don't know if I will ever see my family again. I don't know how to get out of this situation I've gotten into. Help me if you can. I'm a slave with no way to get home. Help me!"

Noah decided to let that be his prayer since he wasn't very good at this praying thing. He tried to sleep but could not. He sat on his pallet and considered all that he could remember about Jehovah God. Why hadn't he listened more closely when the rabbis talked about the prophets, or about how Moses led the Israelites out of Egypt?

With these thoughts tumbling over and over in his head, he finally dozed off and dreamed of his mother and father and the beautiful pastures where he had learned to care for sheep.

Several weeks passed and Noah had not seen William. He knew that many of the slaves were sick, and some had died. He was trying to sleep, but the pallet was hard and uncomfortable. He heard a commotion when the door to his hut burst open and William stood there breathing heavily from his run.

"Come, I need some help."

"What is it?" Noah asked.

"Too many workers have gotten sick for me to care for them alone. I need your help to carry water and help those who are burning with fever. I'll show you what to do. Hurry now!" William turned and disappeared.

Noah quickly put on his tunic and ran to catch up with William.

"Please tell me what to do. All I know is how to care for sheep when they are sick." He was panting in his effort to keep up with William.

"Keep giving them water and cold compresses for the fever. Just make them comfortable. I'll try some of my medicines, then I'm going to see some other sick ones."

William led him to the first hut, and there was an awful odor that was leaking out of the opening. He peaked inside and saw that the inhabitants were not able to keep things clean. They were lying on filthy pallets and were burning with fever. He began by getting a fresh jar of water from the well. He gave everyone sips of water before starting to clean up the trash left by this sick family. By morning, they were sleeping quietly with fresh clothing and water close by.

William came by and pointed him to another hut. Again, he got fresh water, cloths to cool their fever; he swept and cleaned the huts before starting on another. Two days passed as he went from hut to hut helping the sick. He had no sleep, nor had he stopped for food. He was too weary to go another step when William stopped by.

"You have done well, Noah. The worst is over. I could not have done this without you. Go get some food and rest and we will talk more later."

He did not have to be urged as he needed sleep more than food. He slept until the next day, then ate a huge breakfast provided by William. When he had eaten, William sat by him with a thoughtful expression on his kind face.

"Noah, you did a great job with our sick ones. I need someone like you to help me. We have too many people for me to care for alone. I know that you don't know much about healing, but if you are interested, I have some scrolls my wife left that may help you learn more about how to use herbs and poultices. She was a great healer and knew a lot about those things. What do you think?" He inquired.

"Yes, I am interested!" Noah exclaimed. He could hardly contain his excitement. Here was something he could do. Finally, all the years of working with the rabbis was paying off. Unlike so many slaves, he could read and would be able to learn what was in William's scrolls.

"I'll see you tonight." William smiled and laid his arm across Noah's shoulders. "Yes, my son, you do have gifts."

That night he finished his evening meal and hurried to William's hut. There in the back room were rows and rows of scrolls that he had never seen before. The parchments were old and dry and would require extra care. William picked one out and said, "Here, start with this one. When you finish it, come back and I'll give you another."

Chapter 5

Noah couldn't wait to begin learning about healing. Most of the scrolls had been written many years ago with outdated language, and cracks where they had dried out, but he was able to understand them. He wondered if the foliage that grew nearby would be a treasure of herbs he could use for the sick ones. The scrolls even told him some of the symptoms for which they could be used. Late into the night, he read and wondered how he could ever learn all he needed to know to help William.

He need not have worried about such things as the next morning, William arrived at his hut before dawn and roused him out of sleep.

"Come, Noah, you have a new job today. I've cleared it with the master. No more gathering grain for you. You must help me with the sick, and we have many sick ones here. There is a guard with a broken bone first and then a child with fever. Follow me."

William turned and rushed out even before Noah had found his clothes for the day. He followed William who rushed headlong toward the fields where slaves were already at work setting up the grain for threshing. Noah cringed as he passed the threshing stone remembering his beating that first day, but William marched on with determination for the task. They found the guard lying on the ground, writing in pain, with several slaves trying to keep him still. He could see a bone sticking out of the man's leg and his blood was soaking the ground beneath him.

William went to him and gently elevated the leg and whispered soft words to him. Noah tried to remember some of the healing herbs he had read about, but his mind was a blank. Instead, he went to William with intentions of helping, but as he got closer, he realized who the man was—none other than Enoch. The man responsible for his beating. He wanted to run, to rage against this man who almost killed him. How could he help this awful man? But William acted as calm as always, just lifted Enoch's injured leg, and began to gently remove the clothing and asked for clean water.

"Noah, come here. I need you," William called to him.

The time had come for him to decide. Could he contain his rage at this man, or would he walk away? Taking a deep breath and clearing his mind of his anger, Noah managed to say, "I'm here. What can I do?"

"Gently pull on his foot as hard as you can. Here like this," as he showed Noah how to put one hand on top and one on the bottom of his leg and apply pressure. He had never seen an injury as bloody as this one, but he did just as William said. He pulled the leg just a little at first, then pulled harder and harder, until he heard a crunch and the bone disappeared back into the leg. Enoch bellowed and fainted away.

"Okay, now stop," William commanded.

Noah stopped but held on to the leg until William finished wrapping it tightly. Then together they lifted Enoch onto a cart and carried him back to his hut. By this time Enoch had started groaning and thrashing about. From a pouch at his side, William got some leaves, put them in water, and gave the mixture to Enoch to drink. Before long, he had fallen into a restless sleep. William moved quickly to apply a splint of wood and gave instructions to Enoch's friend to come get him if Enoch became so restless that they would be unable to manage him.

Next William went to see the little daughter of one of the slaves. Her parents had become frantic when she was feverish all night. She had long flowing auburn hair which hung in limp strands down her back. One arm was looped tightly around her mother's neck while her other hand clutched her mother's hand. Her parents said that she was difficult to arouse, nor had she had anything to eat or drink all night.

The Healer

William listened and gently ran his hands over her hot skin. When her name was called, she did not awaken. Quickly, William called for cool water and began bathing her. He continued with the cool bath until she aroused and drank some water. He made an elixir from the herbs in his satchel and gently held it to her lips to drink. When William was called away, he instructed Noah to continue the cool baths and to give the elixir.

All night and into the next day, Noah kept refilling the basin and applying the compresses to her forehead and giving the elixir as directed. But no matter how many times he did so, the child continued to worsen. Her fever did not subside, and she no longer cried when moved. When she would not arouse to take the medicine, it became clear that they were not going to be able to save her. He called for William who came at once.

"It's not working, Will. What can we do?"

"There is nothing more we can do. She has not responded to the things I know to do. We need an experienced physician like Dr. Luke, who is the only one I know. He is a Gentile who follows Jehovah. He might be able to help, but he is probably in Jerusalem. He would never get here in time to save her."

Into the night, William and Noah stayed by her side, trying to keep her cool. But before the sun rose, she was gone. At the precious age of three, she would never see the sun rise. The cries of her parents were heard throughout the compound as they ripped their garments and cried loudly. He felt helpless and knew William did also. If only they had known what to do or had someone to help them. He didn't like that helpless feeling and wondered what it would take to find Dr. Luke.

The next day Enoch too was raging with fever. He was yelling out, refusing to allow anyone to look at his injured leg. With his great strength, he was a danger to all his friends who tried to help. William calmly gave him more of the leaves in water so that they could change the bandage. When he removed the bandage, there was a foul odor with a green discharge dripping out of the bloody wound. William washed the wound, placed some different leaves on a bandage, wet it with water, and wound it tightly around the leg.

"This is all I can do for him," William told Enoch's friends. "I just hope it's enough."

"Enough for what?" They asked.

"Enough to save the leg," William replied. "Many times, we have to saw off the leg to save his life. Enoch would not want us to do that."

With instructions to Enoch's faithful friends on how to use the leaves, William left enough for the night.

As Noah and William left Enoch's hut, they heard the friends discussing how they would care for Enoch if he got worse or what they would do if his leg had to be cut off. How would they handle this man who had such great strength? How would they keep him quiet enough to let the leg heal?

Noah wondered too how anyone so injured could have such strength, but he remembered the stinging blows he received and how much strength Enoch had. He even thought it might be better if he died. He had no doubt that Enoch enjoyed hurting people, so maybe this injury was a punishment for his evil ways. He knew he needed William's loving attitude to keep caring for this man.

The next morning, Noah and William went back to Enoch's hut and found him more peaceful. He was anxious to find out what William had used to keep him calm.

"Tell me what was in those leaves," Noah asked.

"They are a mixture of some plants my wife used to help our sick feel better. It's a mixture of ginseng, kava leaves, and poppy seeds. I've experimented with making some of it myself, but I don't have the amounts right. I'm almost out of the samples my wife made," William replied. "I would sure like to make some of it myself, but I don't have the time or the plants. What are you thinking, Noah?"

"Do you think we could get permission for me to go hunting for more?" Noah asked.

William faced him in wonder. "Do you really think you can find more?"

"I don't know, but I'd like to try." He had seen the green forest on his cart ride to the compound and wondered if the needed herbs grew there. The only way to find out would be to go in search of them, but only with the master's permission.

"Then, let me talk to the master. We'll get you the permission you need."

The next morning, William came rushing in and excitedly announced that Noah had permission to be gone two days to find the herbs needed for the compound. He stressed to Noah that the master was trusting him with this job, and he must not fail. He must return within the two days, or the punishment would be severe. Noah assured William that he could be trusted and would return in two days. He gathered his cloak, a skein of water, some bread, and dried meats, and packed them securely in a bundle that he could carry over his shoulder. He also took a spare sack he would fill with his herbs.

Before the sun had cleared the horizon, he set off into the woods. He knew which direction the mountains lay, and he could read the stars, so he was not afraid of getting lost. He was more afraid of wild beasts that might attack since he had no sword to protect himself; his only weapon was a slingshot he had practiced with while watching the sheep with his father. It had been a long time since he had used the slingshot and he hoped he remembered enough to protect himself.

All day he walked and searched for the herbs he had seen in the scrolls. He stayed in the deeper woods as that would be where he could find the ones William used to ease pain. He found some goldenseal, ginseng, echinacea, St. John's wort, plus some that he did not have names for. He gathered some wild mushroom in hopes they would be useful for healing. All the while he kept a close eye for any wild animals. Once he saw a wild boar which would make a good dinner, but he decided it was too heavy to carry home.

After searching all day, Noah was tired as he pulled out his food and drank some cool water from the nearby stream. With a bed of moss and leaves, he lay down thinking of all the ways he would be able to use his precious cargo. As he drifted off to sleep, he realized for the first time in many months he had this new feeling in his heart. Was it joy? Or peace? It must be some of both plus a deep satisfaction that he was doing something useful for the first time ever. He remembered Joseph and his dreams. Could his herbs be the way to get his freedom?

He trudged back into the compound the next day, loaded down with his herbal treasures. He immediately went to wash and separate them, making sure they were not mixed. He hung them together as William instructed, making sure he knew how each would be used. William also helped him with some that he could not name. Together they worked late into the night, carefully setting out any weeds or broken plants. They placed the mushrooms in a separate container to use as an experiment with the sick.

Within the week, the plants had started to turn brown. Noah watched over them to make sure no one changed them around or decided to use them. William had warned him that some people would try to steal them to sell. They were committed to preserving these herbs for the sick and wounded of the farm.

Between visits to the sick, Noah worked on organizing the herbs. William showed him how to extract the syrup from the poppy plants and preserve the seeds. These he carefully placed in a dish to be locked away against thieves. He placed the herbs for skin diseases together, and the ones for coughs and fevers he kept close by for their frequent use.

On his rounds the next day, he had to stop to see Enoch. Noah dreaded this task because he wanted to curse Enoch and rage of how badly he had hurt him, but William had warned him to stay quiet. This was not the time or place to have that discussion.

Enoch was sitting out in front of his hut when Noah arrived. He was using a walking stick to get around, but the leg was healing well.

"Hey, Noah," Enoch asked. "Couldn't wait to gloat and see me hobble around?" "No, I came to see if your leg was healing well."

"It's healing okay, but I know you want to say something else." Enoch looked him in the eye. His haughty look was replaced with a bit of shame. He spoke with a tone of regret in his voice that Noah had never heard from him before.

Here was his chance to say what he needed to say. He leaned over at eye level with Enoch and said, "I need to tell you how much you hurt me the day after I arrived, Enoch. You could have killed me, and I had done nothing to deserve it. Nothing! You set me up on that thresher that you knew I could not move. It's not right that people get treated that way." Noah wanted to strike out at him, but William's warning came to mind.

"Yes, I know what I did." Enoch looked down and frowned. "You and William took good care of me, and you could have refused to help. I owe you for that."

Noah was dumbstruck. This "apology" was so unexpected. Was this the same man who almost killed him for no reason? Could it be that this healing ministry would benefit him in ways he never imagined? He remembered the story of Joseph and how his gifts had helped him during his slavery. Now he began to understand why William had cautioned him about letting his anger out at Enoch over the beating. He had received much more with his new approach. He knew too that the beatings might continue if he did not speak up.

"That kind of treatment must stop. William says he can make sure you don't do it, but if you are truly sorry, you will quit using the whip on anyone. Get rid of it forever."

Enoch did not respond but looked down in shame. He made no further apology, but at least he listened to Noah and looked ashamed.

Chapter 6

Noah became more independent in his visits and treatments as he read the scrolls and worked with William. He enjoyed the respect he received from the other slaves as well as from William. He began to experiment with his herbs to get the most use from them and was able to help some people, but many still died.

He had made little progress with Daniel. Although he had tried many different approaches to engage Daniel is discussions, the man remained quiet, withdrawn, angry, and refused any offer of friendship. He refused to bathe, talk, or help with cleaning their hut.

Things began to change when Daniel did not show up to work one day and Noah found him shivering on his pallet when he returned that evening. He gave him herbs for the fever, kept cool water to drink, and stayed with him through the night.

For five days, Daniel lingered on the brink of death. Noah never left his side, bringing him medicines for the upset stomach and fever, changing his bed linens, and keeping cool water nearby. His body rejected all food as he went from burning hot to shivers at night. He was incoherent most of the time.

On the sixth day, Noah noticed an improvement. Daniel's body was cooler and his mind cleared. He finally asked for some food, and he even stood for a few moments.

"Why are you doing this for me?" He whispered through his dry throat. "Why would you want to CF my friend? I've never even talked to you in the months you have been here. I never wanted a friend, yet here you are."

"My job as a healer is not just to those who are my friends. I am learning to give aid to anyone who needs it," Noah replied. "William has been teaching me about how a healer works with all kinds of people. I did not like to hear it at first, but now I understand. I even had to care for Enoch when he broke his leg. That was so hard, but I did it. And besides that, we don't have any reason not to be friends. We are in this together."

Daniel remained quiet, returned to bed, and rested for the first time in six days. When he woke, Noah could see his eyes were clear. He took food and sat up talking for several hours. As time for bed approached, he murmured, "Thank you, Noah. I would have died without your help."

"You are welcome, my friend," Noah replied. He smiled as he made ready for bed. A new friend would make his days much lighter.

His skills were truly tested one morning when William sent a messenger for him. He grabbed his bag of herbs and ran to William's hut. There he found William lying on his bed, groaning in pain. His body was hot with fever. His breathing was rapid and shallow. Noah checked him carefully and decided to use some angelica and elderberry, cold compresses for fever, and a single small poppy seed for his pain.

Into the night he kept cold compresses on his brow, changed his linens often, and gave drinks when he could swallow. As dawn broke over the horizon, William was no better. How he wished he had the help of that Dr. Luke he had been hearing so much about. This was his beloved William who had saved his life when he arrived. He ached when William groaned and often had to fight tears when he felt sure William was on the brink of death.

He continued caring for William using the herbs that he knew about. During one of his lucid moments, he even asked William what to use and was able to follow his directions. Daniel was well enough and began to show an interest in Noah's work with the sick. He offered to stay with

William while Noah got some sleep. He even began talking to Noah as a friend, asking pertinent questions about the herbs he was using and what he might do to make William more comfortable. Noah gladly accepted his help when he realized that Daniel was willing to do whatever he was asked to do.

For seven days, William groaned in pain. Noah became frantic to help him. He used every herb available, yet none seemed to make a difference. He knew that if they did not do something soon, William would die. Noah sat outside his hut and looked up at the stars. He remembered the songs sung by King David:

> Praise the Lord, my soul,
>   and forget not all his benefits—
> who forgives all your sins
> and heals all your diseases.[6]

This God that William worshiped said He could heal all our diseases. William needed a miracle to survive this sickness. Maybe this God could provide that as well. He had parted the Red Sea for the Israelites to cross. He shut the mouths of the lions when Daniel was thrown into their den. Maybe He could help his friend William to recover.

He looked at the stars and said, "Jehovah, William needs you. I need you too. I don't know you very well, but William believes in you and needs you now. He is your servant, and I don't know how to help him. Do you think you could bring him one of your miracles?"

He went back and sat singing to William until he fell into a restless sleep. He dozed through the night until Daniel came and relieved him. He was too busy to check on William until late in the next day. It seemed that the whole compound of slaves was sick. All work had stopped with the healthy ones caring for the sick.

After the evening meal, Noah went to William's hut expecting to find him dead. Everything was quiet as he approached. As he entered, he saw Daniel asleep on a mat next to William who was sitting up drinking broth. Noah stood and watched a few moments before William noticed him. Then his mouth turned to a huge smile.

"What did you do, son? I'm feeling so much better. I think I'm going to be okay."

"I didn't do anything," Noah replied. He could not describe what had happened last night: the prayer to Jehovah that he wasn't sure he believed in, the crying out for William's miracle. William believed in this God, so that was all that mattered.

"How long have I been sick?" William inquired.

"Seven days. I wasn't sure you were going to live. I can't believe you have made such a remarkable recovery."

"Yes, my friend, it's a miracle," William replied. "Thanks be to Jehovah!"

After that, Noah and Daniel began working together as a team. With the number of slaves increasing, there was enough work for them both, leaving William to recover his strength. They became proficient in caring for injuries, sickness, and childbirths. Working together made life on the farm more satisfying. They could go about their days knowing that a friend was always available to help.

The changes in Daniel were remarkable. He bathed regularly, helped keep their hut neat, joined Noah on his nightly visits to William and often talked late into the night about his life before the farm.

Three Years Later

With the heavy workload on the farm, both Noah and Daniel developed in height and weight. Although Noah was taller, Daniel became stronger with his involvement in the healing work, always able to carry heavy loads when needed. He was no longer the boy who sat huddled in the tent but mingled with the other slaves in the evening or helped with the work of healing.

They learned together from the healing scrolls, discussing the effects of the many herbs they gathered. Although he could not read, he had an inquisitive mind and learned quickly. Noah was surprised to see how Daniel had become a kind and thoughtful healer.

During these talks, Noah and Daniel talked about themselves, their families, and their hopes for freedom. Daniel finally told him the story of his childhood, how he had been abandoned as a small child and had to resort to a life of stealing to survive. He had never known either parent or had ever made friends with another person. He admitted that he did not know how to be a friend, so this was a new experience for him. He learned quickly and discovered that he liked having a friend around. Many times, he demonstrated his loyalty to Noah and the work they did.

One day when William was busy caring for the many slaves, a messenger came from the master that he needed to come immediately. Noah took the message reluctantly since he had never been inside the master's house. William was not present having been called to the far side of the farm. Noah gathered up his bag of medicine and followed the messenger. When he entered the home for the first time, the splendor of the wall hangings and fine furniture amazed him.

But he had no time to gawk, as he was led into the master's chamber where there were fine linens on the bed, rugs from the Orient on the plank floors, and velvet hangings on the walls. There he found the master lying on his bed groaning unintelligible words. He took time to assess his needs as William had taught him. Then he tried his herbal remedies, got a slave to gather towels and cold water, and began to try and reduce the master's fever. He groaned with every movement but seemed to respond to Noah's gentle touch, and by sunset, the master was resting quietly. With things under control with the master, he sent for William.

William was pleased with how well Noah had handled the situation, and together they began the process of making the master comfortable for the night. By morning several more slaves were showing the same symptoms. Noah instructed Daniel on how to manage the many sick slaves, and for the next week, the two men got only snatches of sleep as more and more of the slaves and guards got sick.

By the end of the week, his supplies were running low, but the rate of illness among the slaves was lessening. He had lost two children and one elderly slave, but the others recovered including the master. He was weak and needed assistance, but Noah was able to give instructions to the slaves in his house so he would make a complete recovery.

As things began to settle down after the illnesses, Noah stopped and got some much-needed sleep. Then he reorganized his healing herbs and prepared to obtain more.

With the master on the mend, he got away for two days to resupply his herbs. He knew where to go for each one and developed a system to keep them separated as he found them. He was only gone the allotted two days, but when he returned to the compound, he found a messenger waiting for him.

"You must come to the master's house. He wants to speak to you," the servant said urgently.

"Why?" Noah asked. "Is he ill?"

The Healer

"No," he replied. "You must come. Leave your herbs and come."

Noah carefully left his herb bundles and followed the man. As he entered, the master was seated in the entry courtyard waiting for him. A table was set under the shade of a eucalyptus tree and drinks were prepared with some sweetmeats laid out. The master seemed to be completely recovered.

"Come, Noah," the master said. "I wanted to thank you for all you did and especially for saving my life."

"Uh, you are welcome," Noah stammered. He had never had the master speak so kindly to him.

"Noah, I know that you went beyond what you had to do to take care of us. I have watched you over these years and you have been a faithful servant. You are reliable and good to all my people. I want to repay you for your service. I will give you whatever you desire. If you will tell me what you want, I can make it happen for you," the master looked at him with kindness.

Noah could not think. What should he ask for? His freedom? Money? As he stood there, the master led him to the table and offered a drink and sweetmeats.

"Take your time and think. Remember I can make it happen for you."

Noah took some delicious drink and sweetmeats and pondered what he should say. He swallowed slowly to give himself time to think. This was a decision that could change his life. What should he ask for? Then, his mind cleared, and he knew what he wanted most in life.

He said, "I want the freedom to go find Dr. Luke. I hear he has been in Jerusalem, and I want to find him and learn from him. I know this is asking a lot, since I was sentenced to five years, but I think I need to know more about healing, and he is the only one who can help me."

The master's face showed surprise and awe, and even respect. He sat there a few minutes and then calmly stated, "Son, you have chosen well. You have shown great wisdom in looking to the future. You have served me well and I am pleased that you want to learn about healing. I will make it possible for you to go. Be ready to leave in the morning."

With that, he rose and walked into his house, and Noah was left standing in the shade with the feast before him and the beauty of the farmland surrounding the house. He did not know what to do. His first thought was to inform William. Together they celebrated into the night with tales of Joseph and his multicolored coat, David and his sheep before he became King, and Moses on the mountain getting the laws from Jehovah, and finally Noah told them about the baby.

Noah had never told anyone about the night they saw the messengers, but tonight with William, he told his story. He knew that William would not ridicule him about seeing angels. Instead, William sat and listened intently, then began asking questions.

"So, what did the angels look like? Did they have wings?" He asked.

"No, they looked like you and me but did not touch the ground. And one of them came very close to us and said he had a message for us."

"What was the message?"

"He said we would find a baby lying in a manger in Bethlehem. He said it was good news for all men."

Noah tried to remember all the message, but it was so long ago. "Did you see the baby? What was he like?"

William was leaning forward and staring at Noah waiting for him to reveal a deep truth. He thought back to that night and tried to remember everything.

"We did find the baby, just as the messenger said. My father kept saying, 'This is the One!' But I'm not sure what he meant. We were in a cave-like structure and there were animals all around. The baby's mother was there talking to my father about a message she had received. I wish I had listened more closely."

"Tell me more about the baby."

"I'm trying to remember; it was so long ago. He was just like any normal baby except he was different. I can't explain it. My papa knelt down beside the feeding trough and worshiped him. He seemed to know immediately that this baby was special."

William sat quietly for a long while. Then he said, "Jehovah promised the prophet Isaiah, a savior hundreds of years ago. Many people stopped believing this promise because so much time had passed. But when Jehovah promises something, no matter how long it takes, it is going to happen. That must be what your father meant. That Savior has come not as a soldier, but as a baby. How I wish I could have seen that baby."

After that, William sat in silence and Noah fell silent too. He remembered the baby and thought he would ask his father more when, or if, he ever saw him again.

The next morning, Noah gathered his meager possessions, some food, and a water skein, bade William and Daniel goodbye, and set off down the road toward home. He had no idea how long it would take, but he knew that he could make it. There was one stop he had to make before starting his search for Dr. Luke.

PART II

Freedom

Chapter 7

He thought it would take a week to get home. He could have made it sooner, but the first few days were beautiful days to walk and enjoy his freedom. He was finally free to do whatever he wanted to do. He got a few rides on oxcarts, but mostly he walked. The road was still dusty and rutted from oxcarts. He knew he had to head north and that the flat plains would turn to hill country as he got closer to Jerusalem. He explored the hillsides and forest for the herbs he could use, but he enjoyed most of all the coolness of the shade. He had grown even taller in the years he had been away, probably a head taller than his father. He had a full beard and hair the hung to his tunic collar. His body was strong and muscled, no longer a boyish physique. He wasn't sure if his family would even recognize him.

His family—what would they think of him? He had disappeared without a trace. Would they presume he was dead? Had they searched for him? He felt guilt and shame for what they had endured these years he had been away. Would they welcome him home, or would the shame be too much for them? As he thought of them, he remembered their loving nature, how they had been willing to help neighbors and friends. Widows and orphans could always find help from his mother. No, he had no reason to fear. They would welcome him home.

On his third day out, he noticed several young travelers behind him. He had seen travelers along the way, so he was not worried about these men. He was strong and fit from the years on the farm. As the young men approached, they began asking questions.

"Who are you?" One asked.

"Where are you going?" Said another.

"My name is Noah, and I'm heading to my home in Bethany," he responded.

Before he could utter another word, one man grabbed him around the neck, the other jerked his food bag and water skein. They began to punch and kick him, in the arms, in his ribs, in his legs. Noah tried to defend himself, but they were experienced in this trade. They knew just what to do to disable him. With a final blow to the head from a rock, Noah's knees buckled, and he fell to the ground, while the men continued to kick him. Finally, the darkness came, and he knew no more.

When he woke, he could feel the grass and weed underneath him and the pain. He hurt all over. He tried to move his legs, but they screamed with every movement. His head was covered in something wet, and when he touched it, his hands came away red with blood. When he tried to sit up, his head swam, and the pain traveled forward to his eyes, making his surroundings blurred. He lay back and let the darkness return.

The next time he woke, it was much later in the day. The sun was low on the horizon, and it was getting cooler. His ragged clothes were not protecting him from the cold and his cloak was gone. His food and water were gone. As he lay there, hidden in the tall grass, he wondered how he could get help. He did not think he could be seen from the road due to the tall grass, so he would have to help himself. He began to drag himself toward the road. Each movement was agony as he reached forward to go a little further. He had to get closer to be seen by a traveler. The sun was much lower when he approached the edge of the grass and could see the road again.

He heard travelers along the road as he lay there, but no one had stopped to help. The next time he heard someone, he thought it must be a traveler in a carriage because he could hear the crunch of the wheels on the dirt path. He raised his head and saw a carriage with a tasseled canopy covering the driver. A large black horse pulled the carriage as they bounced along. Noah looked at the carriage and knew that this driver would not stop for him. He must be a rich businessman to have such a fine carriage. He lay back in the grass and felt like crying for the first time since his beating by Enoch. How

The Healer

would he ever get help? He could hear the carriage get closer and then it stopped. He heard the horse blow air and relax. Then a man leaned over him and said, "Hey, can you hear me? Do you need some help?"

"Yes," Noah croaked. "Help me... thieves." That was all he could utter. "Here, let me help you up," the stranger said.

With that, the man leaned down and gently placed his hands under Noah's arms and helped him stand. He wasn't sure he could walk, but with some effort, he discovered that his legs still worked. Slowly and leaning heavily on the stranger, they made their way back to the carriage. He was surprised that this man was strong enough to help him into the carriage, but they were able to get him seated in the soft seat, and the stranger joined him.

Noah could finally look at him. He was a dark-skinned man, with silver hair and beard, long linen cloak, and a jewel on his turban. This man was no slave.

"Who are you?" Noah asked.

"My name is Topek, and I have come from Jerusalem where I go to worship and do business. I am headed home and will take you with me if that is all right with you," he responded.

'Yes, of course. Thank you for helping me. I thought no one was going to stop and help."

"You looked like you could use a little help," Topek chortled. He clicked his tongue, and the horse responded immediately.

Before nightfall, they pulled into the home of this stranger. It was a well-appointed home of stone and planks, a large stone-paved courtyard, and shade trees of figs and eucalyptus. One could travel the road and never see this lovely home set back and tucked into this grove of trees. Topek helped him down and into the cool, immaculate house. He laid him onto a clean bed. Then with practiced hands, he began to wash his wounds and provided Noah with a clean tunic. They decided that he had no broken bones, but bruises covered his body; each breath hurt his chest and his head still hurt, his eyes would not focus, and he had trouble standing. Topek gave him a sleeping elixir and soon he slept.

The next day, Topek continued to care for him. He got delicious food that morning, new dressings on his wounds, then plenty of sleep. It still hurt to take a deep breath, so Noah stayed in the comfortable bed for the day.

"I guess you don't have to do this very often," Noah said that evening as they ate their meal.

"Oh, yes, I do. Those thieves are well practiced in stealing food and money from travelers. You should not have been out there by yourself. What were you doing out there all alone?" He asked.

Noah told Topek his story of how he had been enslaved for his boyish prank. He told of his healing ministry at the farm and how he had just been set free to return home and continue his healing. Topek listened and nodded.

"When you are better, I'll make sure you can get there safely. Did you lose anything valuable?" He asked.

"Only my food and water," Noah replied. "I had no money, but I had collected some valuable herbs along the way. They destroyed those."

"At least you escaped with your life. Sometimes these thieves kill travelers when they think they can get away with it," Topek told him. "You are safe now."

For the next week, Noah rested as the bruises turned green then yellow. Topek kept providing hearty meals, and he could feel his strength returning. He took short walks among the gardens and enjoyed the figs that could be picked from the ground. They sat in the courtyard and talked of many things. Topek had experience with healing but was interested to know more of Noah's experiences.

On his second week with Topek, Noah was wondering about this man who had risked so much to help him. "So, you go to Jerusalem to worship. Why, since you are a Gentile?"

"I go to that Holy City to honor the God of the Jews. I came to faith in that God a few years ago when a man of faith met me and shared with me this Jehovah God. I've been reading the holy scriptures ever since that day. What about you? Do you worship him? As a Jew, you must follow your God?" Topek was looking at him so earnestly, Noah had to look away.

"I'm a Jew, yes, but I can't say I worship Him. I've never felt much like I needed Jehovah. My father is a follower, and he believes."

"I don't think that will help you much, Noah," Topek responded. "From what I've read, you must believe as an individual. Even your forefather Abram had to believe what God told him:

Abram believed the Lord, and he credited it to him as righteousness.[6]

I think you will have to decide someday whether you want to be a follower. You won't be able to stay in the middle of this road for much longer. That day is coming soon, I think, very soon."

Topek got up and turned to Noah. "I'm going back to Jerusalem tomorrow. If you are ready, you may go with me."

"Yes, I will," Noah replied. He was now anxious to be home among his family. Topek's home was a safe place to recover, but he was ready to be home.

The next morning, he donned a clean tunic, and with no belongings of his own, he boarded the carriage. They traveled at a swift pace, but the nice carriage made the journey smooth, and they arrived in Jerusalem by noon. Noah was grateful for a strong animal to get them up those rutted hills to Jerusalem. As he got down from the carriage, he turned to Topek.

"Thank you for all you have done. If you ever need anything, come to Bethany to the house of Zeb and Sarah where you will be welcome."

"You are welcome, my new friend. Go in peace." Topek then turned the carriage and headed back toward Jerusalem.

Chapter 8

Noah turned toward Bethany on the road that was as familiar to him as the lines on his hands. The discussion with Topek had given him much to think about, but today he wanted to think about home. The familiar houses and shops along the way told him that he was drawing near.

As he rounded the last bend in the road, he saw his mother in the courtyard tending the chickens. He stopped and watched as his heart filled with love for her. She now had silver streaks in her hair and her walk was a bit slower, but he would recognize her anywhere. She was the most beautiful woman he had ever seen. The sweet pure notes of the song she sang filled his heart with memories of days long ago. Then he saw another woman standing nearby. Who could that be? As he watched her walk toward his mother, he realized that it was Miriam. She too had grown into a beautiful woman, with dark hair and a pouty lip. Her confident walk and strong arms told him that she was a woman of substance

He stood there until his mother turned and saw him. She stopped her work and stared at him, waiting. When recognition hit her, she burst into a loud shout. "Noah, is that you?" She started running toward him, jumped into his arms, and embraced him before he could even respond.

"Oh, my son! I've been so worried for you. I've prayed for you every day! Come inside, your father will be home soon, and he will be so thrilled. Tell me everything."

She grabbed him and would not turn him loose as she dragged him into the familiar home he had missed so much. She scurried about and prepared fresh tea to drink and food to eat. She would not stop talking, so he just enjoyed the sound of her voice, the familiar smell of his home, and the hint of jasmine he remembered from his mother's bosom.

He ate everything his mother brought, and finally she stopped and asked, "Where have you been? Rocco told us that the guards took you away, but we did not know where they had taken you. We were so worried about you, but we prayed every day."

"Wait until Papa gets home, and I will tell you everything," Noah replied.

He didn't want to have to tell his story multiple times, so he just sat and enjoyed the cool of the day and got reacquainted with his mother and sister.

Just then the door burst open, and his father rushed in. "Miriam said you were home," as he grabbed Noah into a bear hug.

The familiar smell of his father filled him with such joy, he could only stand and stare at this man who had aged but was still the loving Papa he remembered. His hair had turned silver gray and he was slightly stooped. His voice was still strong with the tones Noah remembered as he would fall asleep as a child.

After many hugs, they sat, and he told his story. He left out the part about the beating so he could spare his parents the pain he had endured. He told them of William and how he took such good care of the slaves. He told of learning the art of healing and his experience of taking care of the master when he became ill. Then he told them of his encounter with the thieves on the road and showed them his bruises which were still visible. He told them of Topek who had risked his own safety on the road. How he made sure he got home safely. On into the night they talked of the years Noah had been away, of the things he had learned and the kindness of the master.

"How did you get released?" His papa finally asked.

"When the master became ill, I helped him. With so many slaves ill, I was the one to care for him. He eventually recovered and gave me permission

The Healer

to leave so that I might find Dr. Luke that I've heard so much about. I hear he is in Jerusalem, and I hope to find him. I can't stay here very long because the doctor can help me learn more of the healing art." Noah wanted to let them know his plans so they would not start making plans of their own.

"Maybe I can help," Papa countered. "I've heard of this physician, who is a Gentile, but he heals any who need him. I'll ask my friends if they know where to find him."

Noah felt the same companionship he had felt as a child as he saw his father and mother supporting his decision to go to Jerusalem. They talked of other ways they could help him. They offered their home as his home base whenever he needed them. No longer a boy, he began to feel like the man he had become. His years of slavery were over, and he had managed to become a healer. There was so much he wanted to say to his father, but that would have to wait until tomorrow. For now, his exhaustion had surfaced. He needed to sleep in his own bed with his family nearby and wake to the sound of their busy household. Even Miriam could not bother him tonight. He slept soundly in the bed of his childhood, dreaming of finding the doctor everyone was talking about.

He woke to the familiar sound of the chickens and goats in the courtyard and his mother cooing to them as she spread grain. Mariam was already hanging clothes to dry in the hot Judean sun. Today, Noah would have to get organized for the search for Dr. Luke. It would not be easy, since Jeruselam was a big city so Noah would need a plan to find one Gentile doctor.

The next two days passed quickly. Noah prepared his sack with food and some healing herbs he had been able to purchase at the market. His father's friends mentioned several places Dr. Luke was known to practice his trade around Jerusalem. He even had a contact for a person who might have a room to spare. When everything was ready, he said "goodbye" and walked out of town alone. He was hopeful that he might finally meet the man who could help him become the respected healer he wanted to be.

The first day in Jerusalem, he was in awe at the busy streets, the bustling merchants, the many languages he heard. He searched for anyone who

55

knew Dr. Luke, but no one did. He found the room where he could stay, and with money from his father, he paid for the month.

Day after day, Noah walked the streets of Jerusalem. He tried the healing pools, the temple courts, the marketplace, but he could not find anyone who knew Dr. Luke. He wondered if he applied his healing art where he was needed, then maybe Dr. Luke would find him.

One day as he was walking the streets, a chariot raced by with a second chariot close behind. As they passed him, one of the drivers took a sharp turn to pass the chariot ahead of him, when the horse revolted at the maneuver. The driver flew over the side and landed on the road in a heap. All the onlookers stood watching, but none offered their assistance. He was a Roman soldier, after all, so no Jewish person was going to help.

Noah walked to him and calmly knelt to help. Blood was running from his mouth and from a large wound on his leg. He was not responding to commands, and his face was pale as a cloudy day. Noah knew the man was seriously injured, and knowing he would need some help, he spotted a man nearby who looked like he might be a slave and called to him for help. The man turned and did not seem to understand his language, but he recognized the situation. Together he and Noah picked up the injured man and carried him to the nearest inn.

Noah began by checking for other wounds, and finding none, he decided to try the technique that William had taught him. The soldier was thrashing about on the bed, yelling out so much the stranger was having trouble holding him. Noah realized the need to relieve his pain first before they could do anything, so he found some poppy seeds and gave him one with some sips of water.

After an hour, he was still screaming in pain, so Noah gave him another seed. Finally, the man calmed, and the stranger could hold him still enough for Noah to pull on the leg until he heard a crunch. The Roman screamed in pain, writhing, and pulling on his clothing. Noah was thankful that the helper remained calm and kept the soldier still while he fashioned a splint of wood, bandaged the wound, then checked his work. He explained

The Healer

the situation to the innkeeper and reassured him he would return the following day. He needed more supplies as this man's recovery would be a hard one. He turned to the stranger and said, "Thank you for your help." He didn't know if the man understood him, but the stranger nodded and walked away.

Noah headed straight to the market to search for his healing herbs. As he scoured the vendors, he saw a crowd gathered around a crippled man. He drew closer and noticed another man standing apart but nearby. He watched as this stranger gently placed his hand on the crippled man and ran it over his body. He touched the man's arms, then his legs, and placed both hands on his head. The crippled man sat quietly and boldly answered his questions.

After a short while, the stranger moved on to the next couple. They had a small child in their arms. She was a little girl much like the child so many years ago who had died despite all Noah could do to save her. She had the same auburn hair, the same grip on her parents, and the listless expression. He often thought of this child and what her life would have been like if he had been able to save her. He watched as the stranger took the child and gently gave her some liquid to drink. Then he returned the child to the parents, gave them instructions on her care, and then moved on to the next person.

Noah watched all afternoon as this stranger cared for the sick and wounded. He stayed on the outside of the crowd to avoid being noticed. What was he seeing? He continued observing this man who always seemed to know what to do. He was completely unflappable, confident, and so gentle. He was watching a new approach to the sick, when he saw how the man used his hands as eyes to look into his patients' illnesses.

As the crowd thinned and the sun began to set, it became more difficult to remain unnoticed, so he left, determined to come back the following day.

He returned to the inn and found the soldier in great pain. He administered the poppy seeds and tried cool compresses. He used some ginseng and elderberry wine and some oils on his wounds. After several hours, the soldier quieted and was able to rest.

Noah sat by the bed and thought about the healing stranger he had seen that day. Maybe this stranger could help him with the Roman. Or maybe he might know where Dr. Luke could be found. Noah had never seen such techniques before. He had a spirit about him that Noah could not identify but wanted to know more. Meanwhile he had this Roman soldier to care for and did not know what more he could do. His injuries might be more severe than Noah could handle alone.

The next day, Noah returned to the marketplace, but there was no healer. He searched and searched, but no one could help. Finally, he gave up and started back to the inn. He passed the palace of the high priest that stood only slightly lower than the temple, and then there was the beautiful temple which had been rebuilt many years before. He noticed a crowd had gathered by the front gate. He knew Dr. Luke was a Gentile, so he would not be in the Jewish temple.

As he drew closer, he saw that same stranger talking to the sick. He watched as he placed healing herbs on wounds, set some broken bones, and gave medicines to the feverish. With each patient, he stopped and bowed his head to pray. Noah stayed until the crowd was gone and he could no longer hide the fact that he was standing there gawking at this stranger.

As the last person left, the stranger looked up and said, "Who are you? This is the second time I've seen you watching. Do you need healing?"

Noah remained silent as he rose and walked toward the stranger. Who was this man who spent hours each day healing the sick? He was not performing magic but was listening and caring. He helped all who came to him no matter how long it took. Maybe there was another healer that Noah did not know about.

"My name is Luke," the stranger said. "How may I help?"

Noah's heart gave a quick beat and his breath stopped. Here was the man he had been searching for. "I've been looking for you all over town. My name is Noah and I'm learning the healing art. I would like to come work with you. But first I have a Roman soldier who needs your help. He is seriously injured, and I've already done all I can. Do you think you could come with me to see him? I have much to talk about, but first the soldier needs our help."

Luke turned and immediately gathered his things. "Let's go. I want to hear more."

Together they hurried back to the inn where Dr. Luke gave the Roman a careful examination. He checked the leg and was pleased with the job Noah had done. He reviewed the medicines he had been given and approved of each step. Since the soldier was resting quietly, Noah began his story to the doctor and told him all about his years as a slave and how he had learned the healing arts. He even shared his story of the beating and how he would have died without William's careful attention. He held nothing back. Luke listened and nodded, saying little. When Noah drew silent, Luke looked at him with compassion in his eyes.

"Noah, you have been through a lot, and you have learned well from William. You already know much about the healing arts, but there is more to learn. I am still learning, but I would be pleased to teach you what I know."

Luke leaned in and placed his hand on Noah's hand. He started talking to Jehovah (but he is a Gentile, Noah thought). "O Lord, thank you for this opportunity to teach one of your own. Make us a team that you will be proud of. We want you to have glory from what we do."

Noah didn't know what to say, so he remained quiet. They sat that way for a while with Luke's hand on his. Luke drew quiet also and he noticed that Luke's eyes were moist. What could be going on in his mind? He just wanted to learn what Luke knew, but he began to wonder if there was more to this physician than he had been told.

Noah's training started early the next morning. After checking on the Roman, he followed Luke toward the market, near the place he had seen him earlier. The crowd seemed to know they could find the healer because the sick started showing up. There were those crippled from birth, blind, lame from injuries, sick with fevers, and even demon possessed. Luke did what he could to help, giving each one individual attention. Many could not be helped with their disease, but Luke gave them attention anyway. He never asked for money, yet many left food, supplies, herbs, and money. All expressed thanks and praises to Jehovah when Luke prayed for each patient before he moved on to the next.

Many times, that day, Luke asked Noah his opinion, surprising him as he thought he would be learning from Luke. But in the days to come, he discovered he had much to offer, and they became a team, working long days and nights side by side to help the sick and wounded.

It became a mutual learning for both men, and as the weeks and months passed, they developed a close friendship. They had opportunities to sit and talk about many things. Although Noah was reluctant to talk about his time as a slave, he eventually talked further about the beating that almost killed him. He admitted that he still felt anger at the man, but simply pushed it back whenever their paths crossed at the farm. He shared his concerns for Daniel who was still at the farm, presumably for the rest of his life.

One day as they stopped by a stream to escape the heat of the day, Noah was looking into the crowd and noticed a face he thought he would never see again. He stared at the face and the man stared back at him. Then the man started toward him with a huge smile and grabbed him in a bear hug.

"Noah, is that really you?"

"Rocco, it is me!" Noah cried out in joy. "Where have you been, and what are you doing? I never thought I would see you again."

"Noah, how are you?" Rocco laughed. "I'm so glad to see you. I've wondered so many times where you were and what you were doing."

"I just got home a few months ago. It's a long story about where I've been. First, tell me about you!"

"I've been right here! I heard about this messenger who came out of the desert, and I started following him. His name is John, and he had been in the desert for a long time, so he wears clothes made from camel's hair and a leather belt around his waist. He eats locust and honey, but his message is one that made sense to me. I've never heard anything like it before. It has changed my life completely. He told us that we must all repent because the Kingdom of God is very close. He makes us believe that things are about to change with the coming of a Messiah from Jehovah. You have to come with me to hear him." Rocco was speaking so fast and moving his arms and jumping around as he talked.

"Slow down," Noah replied. "Let me tell you about myself. I have become a healer and I am working with Dr. Luke, so I don't have much time for following a preacher from the desert. Don't you want to know where I have been?"

"Sure, your turn, tell me what happened to you. I was so scared when they took you away. I thought I would never see you again."

Noah told him all about the master's farm and how he survived the many years of slavery. He told Rocco of his struggles with being a slave and of William who had helped him become a healer and how he came back to Jeruselam to search for Dr. Luke. Rocco listened intently, while Noah's old feelings of friendship flowed over him. His years away from Rocco seemed to melt away as they talked. He had a hard time seeing this Rocco as a grown man with dark curls around his face, brown eyes that sparkled in the sun, broad, well- developed shoulders and legs that looked like he could walk all day and not grow weary. The ragged boy who stole food for his family was gone, and in its place was this strong man who talked of the Kingdom of God.

There were more sick people coming, so Noah returned to his task. Rocco stayed close by, helping when he could, but refusing to leave until the sun had set and all the sick had been attended. He helped them clean up, made provisions for dinner, then stayed around to talk.

There was something different about his old friend. Was it the big smile? Rocco never smiled! Was it the easy way of his walk? His demeanor was different for sure. Those eyes were the same but different; they shone with joy and laughter. There was a gentleness about him that Noah could not remember. He too had grown into a man in the years they had been apart. Rocco was not as tall as Noah, but stouter compared to Noah's lean frame.

Rocco joined them as if he had been with them from the beginning, talking into the night about their lives and how things had changed. He never mentioned leaving or being needed elsewhere. Rocco talked the most about this itinerant preacher who was calling everyone to repent. Since Noah did not know what 'repent' meant, Luke joined in to explain that everyone who follows Yahweh God needed to admit their sin and turn away from them and live a different way. Then Rocco talked about how he had done that, and his life had changed. He now worshiped Yahweh God and couldn't stop talking about Him.

As Noah listened, Rocco and Luke talked on and on about this preacher. Luke seemed to know more about him than Noah realized.

As Noah sat and listened, he thought about his life and concluded that he was a pretty good person. The only time he had stolen was when he had gotten caught. He was good to his family, and he treated his friends well. What could he have to repent? He didn't think he had anything to confess. He was still angry at the thieves who hurt him and had stolen his food, but that was completely normal. He still had trouble forgiving Enoch, but they had reached a silent truce before he left the farm. He concluded that he was no worse than any of the other Jewish men he knew. He thought maybe they were taking this message a little too seriously.

Chapter 9

Days later, Rocco was still hanging around while Noah and Luke worked with the sick. He always found something that needed attention whether he was greeting the sick, cleaning up from their day, or obtaining food and lodging. He never complained and was fast becoming a vital part of their team. At the end of each day, he had long conversations with Luke while Noah felt left out. He was interested in what they had to say, but had nothing to contribute and finally, Noah had had enough.

"So, what can an itinerant preacher who dresses funny and has no education say to us?"

"I can't explain it," Rocco replied. "There is something about him that shows he has the authority to be saying these things. He says the Kingdom of God is near and that we should be looking for a Messiah. He has known this man since they were boys, and he is sure that this is the Messiah. Just come with me and see for yourself. I think I know where to find him."

Noah was very skeptical about this but decided that it was the only way to get Rocco to stop talking about the man. The next day, Rocco arrived early and hurried them toward the river where he said that John the Baptizer could usually be found. And there he was, telling the crowd that someone else was coming who was much more worthy than himself. He told them to repent, repent, repent. He was not a handsome man, but his tunic was ragged and dirty, his hair stood on end and stuck out all over his head. His beard had not been trimmed in many weeks.

Rocco and Luke were both mesmerized by this preacher, but Noah held back and thought he would wait and see what the man would do. He wondered if the man was using some magic tricks or sleight of hand to lure people to him. He watched as many people went into the water to be baptized. They all come out laughing and smiling and shouting with joy, praising God. Something was happening, but Noah was not sure he understood what it was. He thought perhaps he should listen more closely when Rocco and Luke were involved in their long conversations.

As it happened, there were many sick among the crowds that gathered for the Baptizer, so Noah and Luke returned several more times. 5IFy would tend the sick and listen to the preacher, then more people would arrive, so their days were long and busy.

As they worked, Luke began to tell him more about this promised Messiah. He told Noah about how he met a man who shared the stories of Jehovah God leading the Israelites out of Egypt. He told about how God saved the Gentile woman, a prostitute named Rahab, even when He destroyed the city of Jericho. She was a Gentile but wanted to follow the God of the Jews. Then Luke said he had concluded this God they worshiped might also save him, a Gentile physician. He had been studying the holy scriptures for himself and even went to the temple sometimes. He could not go with the Jewish men, but still felt he could worship in the outer court. Most often he worshiped alone by the roadside or sitting in the shade.

"I'm telling you, my friend, this God is real. I can't explain the whole thing, but what I know about Him has changed me. Noah, I've known you for a good while now, but I've never asked if you trust in Jehovah God?" Luke turned with love and concern in his face.

"I haven't given it much thought. I saw my father trusting in Yahweh when I was a child. Then we saw the messengers that night in the field telling us about that baby He was sending. My father believed He was the One they had been waiting for, but I was doubtful it could be that important. I guess I never thought God cared much about me. I was a slave and God never stepped in and saved me. I've been beaten and nearly died, but God never rescued me. Then I was attacked by those thieves, and I thought I would die for sure. Still God did not help me."

"Oh, but He did, Noah," Luke responded firmly. "You learned such valuable truths while there at the farm. He sent you William to teach you. He saved your life when Enoch beat you. You helped many people with your gifts of healing. He sent you a man to help you when the thieves attacked you. Jehovah never promised us that we would have an easy life, but He promises he will go with us wherever we go. You need to stop feeling sorry for what you went through and start being thankful for what you have been given. He was there with you every step of the way."

With that, Luke turned and began gathering his things and started for home. Luke had never spoken to Noah in that way, and he was reeling from his response. He was left standing and wondering what Luke meant by "being thankful for what he had been given." He had worked hard for what he had, and no one had given him anything. He was just wrong about that. But Luke was his friend and teacher, someone who had shown him a different way to live. He could not be angry with his friend but wondered why he kept coming back to the same story again and again.

A few weeks later, as Noah and Luke were walking among the crowd, they noticed a stranger that neither had seen before. The crowds parted and allowed him through, and the men heard "Lamb of God" and "Messiah" whispered as he passed. The strangest thing was how John the Baptizer was acting. He stopped preaching, stood still, and fixed his gaze on this man who indicated that he too wanted to be baptized. John kept saying, "No, no, I should be baptized by you."

But the stranger insisted. "Do it. God's work, putting things right all these centuries, is coming together right now in this baptism." So, John did it.[7]

Then as he was coming up out of the water, Noah heard a voice saying, *"This is my Son, chosen and marked by my love, delight of my life."*[8] Then he looked toward the voice and saw the sky open up and what looked like a dove came down and rested on him. That voice was like nothing else, yet familiar. Where had he heard that voice before? It brought back memories from long ago. That voice brought memories of a feeding trough and a baby's gentle cry."

Noah could only stand there with his mouth open, but all around him, people were falling on their knees and worshipping this man. Even his friends were kneeling as if in prayer. How could they worship someone they had never seen before? But that voice he heard was one he knew. It was on the night he saw the baby. It was the same loud voice, and it caused the same sensations in his stomach. What could this mean? That voice, with so much authority, such power. Where did it come from? Luke and Rocco would know more, and he needed to start paying closer attention when they talked in hushed whispers.

"Where did that voice come from?" Noah finally asked

"He is the promised one. That was the voice of His Father, Jehovah God. The prophet Isaiah wrote that we would get a Savior," Rocco said, "*So, the Master is going to give you a sign anyway. Watch for this: A girl who is presently a virgin will get pregnant. She'll bear a son and name him Immanuel (God-With-Us).*"[9]

"And Isaiah also promised,

> *For a child has been born—for us!*
>   *the gift of a son—for us!*
> *He'll take over*
>   *the running of the world.*
> *His names will be: Amazing Counselor,*
>   *Strong God,*
> *Eternal Father,*
>   *Prince of Wholeness.*
> *His ruling authority will grow,*
>   *and there'll be no limits to the wholeness he brings.*
> *He'll rule from the historic David throne*
>   *over that promised kingdom.*
> *He'll put that kingdom on a firm footing*
>   *and keep it going*
> *With fair dealing and right living,*
>   *beginning now and lasting always.*
> *The zeal of God-of-the-Angel-Armies*
>   *will do all this.*"[10]

The Healer

Rocco continued, "You remember that baby you told us about. This is He, that same man. God told you and the other shepherds that he would be sent for all humanity. He would be our Redeemer -- to buy us back out of our slavery. And that voice, was the voice of his Heavenly Father."

Noah was amazed that Rocco knew so much about this promised Messiah. Something had really changed him in the years they had been apart. But he could not deny that the change was good. Rocco no longer went on his outings to steal food, and he treated Noah with respect and dignity. He smiled frequently and moved with confidence in himself. He was kind to the sick that came as well as to all the families. He was always singing praises to Yahweh, the Almighty One.

"So, you think this man, Yeshua, is that promised One, the Messiah?" Noah continued.

"I do," Rocco replied without hesitation. "John is sure of it, and I believe him. I've been listening to him for many months, and he makes a lot of sense to me. I know that I'm a changed man from the one you knew from childhood. You must know that I have changed. We can watch him together and make sure if you still have doubts."

"I do need to see more for myself. If he is really the promised One, he will start his own army and we can join up. Israel really needs a deliverer now."

"I don't think that is what He is going to do. He doesn't look like a warrior. I think the war he is fighting is a different kind," Rocco replied. "His war is for the hearts of men and women." It didn't sound like Rocco wanted to fight anyone right now.

Chapter 10

As was his custom, Luke traveled all around the area to reach the sick and, together with Rocco, they made their way north to Nazareth. It took several days to make the journey. The smooth road of the Romans turned into a rutted, dirt path that wound through hills and valleys bordered by caves frequented by robbers. Rocco warned them to be alert as they walked lest they be attacked by thieves. He had fallen into the role of securing supplies for them and making sure they had a place to stay at every stop since he knew the area well. Now he became their guard.

As they were walking on the road, it was not unusual for them to meet travelers along the way. Luke usually initiated conversations with them, and Noah and Rocco would fall behind to laugh and talk of old times. Luke had met two men that day and was enjoying his visit while they walked and talked about the political situation south of the city. Noah thought he heard a voice that jogged a memory. He turned to the strangers and stopped to listen. He noticed something familiar about them. It wasn't in their appearance, but when he closed his eyes a moment and listened to them, he knew he had heard them before. He heard again the yelling they did while they pulled at his cloak and stole his food and water. 5IFTe men had to be the two thieves he had encountered on his way home from the farm. But that couldn't be. These men were well dressed, calm, peaceful businessmen. He looked at them carefully and considered their faces, their size, their walk. Yes, it was the same men.

Anger boiled up in him. How could they act like nothing had ever happened? Were they planning to rob his group of friends? He wanted to tear them limb from limb, rage at them, tear their clothes, hit and kick them like they had hurt him.

Rocco saw his confusion and pain and said, "What's wrong, friend?"

"Nothing!" Noah felt so angry he wasn't sure he could tell his friend about this. "It's not nothing; I see it on your face. Tell me."

"It's the thieves, the same ones who attacked me many years ago. They left me for dead and took my food. They kicked and punched me until I could not walk. How could they so calmly walk up to us and act like nothing ever happened?" Noah was having trouble even saying it aloud.

"Hold on, my friend. Let's make sure."

Rocco moved up to meet them. He listened to the conversation until there was a pause. He turned to the men and said, "My friend back there thinks he knows you. Have you ever met him?"

The two men turned to Noah and paused. They looked him over, then they looked at each other as if to admit their identity. They hung their heads and began stammering their speech.

"Um, we may have encountered you during our days as thieves. We were pretty bad guys until our lives were changed by the Master," they confessed.

"Tell us more," Rocco jumped in when he saw Noah start to protest.

"We ran very wild and hurt many people until we met a man called Yeshua on the road one day. He talked to us and knew everything about us. He told us about a God, called Jehovah, who loved us just like we are. He helped us see how much we were hurting people and that we could be different with the power that He gave. We committed our lives to Jehovah God that day and have never been sorry. Tell us how we hurt you and we will repay you twice over," they said.

"It isn't so much what you took from me, it's how much you hurt me," Noah cried. "I was alone, had nothing of value, yet you punched and kicked me until I almost died. I wanted to come after you and kill you myself, but I met a man who helped me recover. He convinced me that I would not be able to do what I really wanted to do. But I did not forget the pain you caused."

Both men looked down in anguish. "We are so sorry for our behavior. If we could make it up to you, we would. But there is no way to recompense you for that kind of pain. Here take this gold and use it for your ministry," as the two men handed Noah two large gold coins.

Noah did not know whether to take the money or not. He wanted to stay angry with these men, but his hurt and pain seemed to be dissolving as he saw tears in the eyes of the two men. He looked to Luke, who nodded his head and smiled.

Noah reluctantly took the coins and said, "I've had anger at you for a long time. I hope I can feel differently in the future."

With that he turned to walk on ahead, his feelings a big jumble in his chest.

Chapter 11

One day while working in Nazareth, Rocco came running toward them.

"Hurry, come quickly. That man, Yeshua, has shown up in the synagogue. You said you needed to know more, so here is your chance. He is here and they have asked him to speak."

Both Noah and Luke turned to gather their medicines and followed Rocco. They went into the synagogue and Luke hung back in the outer court.

"You go on ahead. I'll wait here."

Noah and Rocco slipped in with the other Jewish men just in time to see the stranger stand up and ask for a specific scroll. He unrolled the scroll and read,

> *God's Spirit is on me.*
> *he's chosen me to preach the Message of good news to the poor,*
> *Sent me to announce pardon to prisoners and*
> *recovery of sight to the blind,*
> *To set the burdened and battered free,*
> *to announce, "This is God's year to act!"* [11]

Then He rolled up the scroll and sat back down. The eyes of everyone were on Him. No one spoke. He continued, "*You've just heard scripture make history. It came true just now in this place.*"[12]

Noah could not believe what he was hearing. That was the scripture he had memorized so many years ago. It was the same man he had seen on the river who was baptized by John the Baptizer.

Rocco sat spellbound during this reading. Noah watched as his friend's face showed surprise, then complete joy at that last statement.

This man was claiming to be God Himself! That did not make sense. How could a man be God? This man, the one who walked, talked, and got hungry, tired, and sleepy. This same man was standing up claiming to be fulfilling scripture. If that was true, then those verses took on new meaning. He decided that this man was indeed turning the Jewish faith upside down and required a more thorough hearing than Noah had given him. Was history really be made by an itinerant preacher from Nazareth? Rocco believed with his whole heart, but Noah wasn't so sure.

In the coming months as Rocco, Luke, and Noah traveled around from Nazareth to Jerusalem, they often spotted that stranger, Yeshua, walking along the Sea of Galilee, or near Jerusalem. He was always surrounded by people and sometimes a big crowd followed. He would stop and teach awhile, then travel on to a quiet place to rest. Often, if Luke stopped near a garden of olive trees to rest, they would see Yeshua resting under a tree with just a small group of men gathered around Him. Always, these men were listening intently to His words. In quiet tones, He sat teaching them about how to treat others, how to be holy, what to do when He left them. Sometimes He would fall to His knees and begin talking to His Father. Noah could hear Him speaking of His children, of heaven, and how He longed to be with His Father.

These things puzzled Noah. Where was this man going? Who was the Father that could talk to Him this way? Who were these children this man spoke of? Noah knew from local gossip that the man was not married and had no children. Maybe He was a mad man. These men who were followers did not seem to think so. Rocco and Luke did not think so either. Both men answered his questions freely, but never pushed him. Luke never spoke harshly again, so Noah continued asking his questions.

The Healer

In the years to follow, this teacher appeared often along their journey to Galilee from Jerusalem. Noah observed times when the teacher stopped to deal with sick ones, and times when he laid hands on someone who was crippled who would stand and walk away. Noah would marvel at the power of the man,, wishing he could heal like that. When he expressed such thoughts, Luke and Rocco would smile and turn away.

Chapter 12

Rocco surprised them when he suggested that he would like to spend Passover with his family. Noah thought it would be a good time to visit his parents and maybe he would find an opportunity to discuss some of the questions that kept coming up since they were seeing this Teacher so often.

Luke, being Gentile, hadn't said much but was agreeable to going back to Jerusalem. As they approached the city, the road got more crowded with visitors coming for Passover. They were jostled and shoved as they tried to make their way into town.

One group shouted louder than the others, "Blessed is the king who comes in the name of the Lord!"

"Peace in heaven and glory in the highest!"

Some of the priests in the crowd said to Yeshua, "Teacher, rebuke your disciples!"

"I tell you," He replied, "if they keep quiet, the stones will cry out."[13]

Noah realized that it was that man, Yeshua, riding on a donkey, going into Jerusalem. As he got closer, he noticed tears in His eyes as He surveyed the city below Him.

Noah turned to Luke and asked, "What does this mean? Why is He riding a donkey, and everyone is calling Him a king, and throwing down cloaks and branches for Him to ride over? If He is a king, shouldn't He have a nice horse? And the man is crying!"

Luke's face became solemn as he replied, "Friend, He must be going into Jerusalem to celebrate the Passover, but the leaders here are not going to allow it. They hate Him so much; I don't know what they are capable of. They've been trying to kill Him for months now and He still came to Jerusalem. I'm not sure why He did that, but it's not safe for Him here."

"But why do they hate Him so much?" Noah asked.

"He has stirred them up because He wants everyone to acknowledge Jehovah God as one God and He is His Son. Remember that baby in the manger? Well, there He is. He wants our religion to be from the heart, not just in our mouths in the synagogue. He wants us to love like His Father loves us. If we loved like that, we would no longer need the priests to make sacrifices for us. Imagine how they would like that?"

Noah thought about it and replied, "Sounds like He wants to turn everything around. No priest, no temple, and no sacrifices. I can't imagine that!"

"Neither can the priests," Luke countered. "They want to continue making sacrifices for us, and Yeshua is claiming that He is the sacrifice. They want to control us politically, but He wants a religion of the heart, not a political one."

"What can they do?"

"I don't know, but it is not going to be easy on Yeshua," Luke replied softly.

Noah could not comprehend what Luke meant but decided it would be best to let it rest. Some things this man was teaching left him with many unanswered questions. He led Luke out toward the edge of the crowd. "There are so many people here, we will never find a place to stay. My parents live a short distance out of town. Let's go there and stay," he suggested.

Since Rocco was going to his mother's house, Luke agreed to the plan, and they set off. Before the sun set, they arrived at the modest home of Zeb and

The Healer

Sarah. They gave Noah many hugs and kisses as they ushered him and Luke into the courtyard.

Noah introduced Luke who was received as a family member. Sarah and Miriam scurried off to start the evening meal while Luke and Zeb launched into a discussion of the political happenings in Jerusalem.

"So, what do you make of this teacher named Yeshua? We saw Him riding into town on a donkey," Luke asked.

Zeb took his time replying as he always did. "I've been following his teachings since that night in the fields when we saw a Messenger from Jehovah. According to the holy scriptures, Jehovah promised a child that would save the world. I believe that He is the One. I just don't know how this is going to happen. I know the priests don't want Him here, and I've heard that they are trying to kill Him. That would be a very sad day for His followers. But I don't know how we can stop them."

"We can't stop it. If He is the One, then He should be able to stop it if God wills." Luke began to pace as he talked. "I heard that He is claiming to be God, so it stands to reason that He could stop the priests if He wanted to."

"I agree," Zeb replied. "I've heard that He has raised the dead, given sight to the blind, and healed some who were crippled since birth. No one has ever been able to do that. You can help some of the sick, but you haven't raised the dead, have you?"

"No, never," Luke agreed. "Sometimes I wish I could, but I've never had that gift."

Dinner that evening was a lively affair. Noah was amazed at how Luke fit into his family. He seemed to draw out Zeb as Noah had never been able to do. He realized that he really did not know his parents well. He had left as a young man who never listened to his parents when they talked of religious matters, so that was all he knew of them. Now that he was an adult, he began listening closer to what his father said. Zeb talked at length about the sacrifices of the priest and how they were to end with the Messiah. He acknowledged that many expected the Messiah to form an army and launch a rebellion against Rome, but he did not think that was supported by the holy writings.

Luke listened intently to all Zeb had to say. He added to the conversation when he could fill in details from his travels. He told Zeb about the baptism of Yeshua at the river Jordan some years earlier.

"John the Baptizer preached about repentance more than sacrifices. Then Yeshua came and asked John to baptize him. Now the Romans have killed John. Why aren't they satisfied with one innocent man's death? This man does not deserve to die either."

"You heard the voice?" Zeb asked.

"Yes, and I did not understand it at the time," Luke replied. "It was a loud sound, then the clouds opened up and the dove came down and sat on his shoulder. We heard the voice say, '*This is my Son, chosen and marked by my love, delight of my life.*'[14] That could only mean one thing. He must be the Messiah."

Noah listened but continued to hold back judgment on the man. He would wait and see if the Jews would stop the priest from killing Yeshua this week. If He was killed, that would settle the question because no one would continue to claim Him King if He was dead.

The week was busy for the two healers. As the crowd grew, so did the sick and injured. Everywhere they went, people came needing their skills. Noah did not have much time for considering Yeshua, called the Teacher, but he saw the man among the crowds as he worked. After the middle of the week, he stopped seeing Him and wondered if something had happened to Him.

On Thursday, Rocco returned to help, but planned to return home for the Passover the next day. The three men were met with rumors that the Teacher had been arrested. The crowds were agitated, running here and there trying to get word of the coming execution. It seemed that the crowds were determined to send Him to die that day, and they could not get enough of the spectacle.

The Healer

While they were walking by the palace, the men noticed that the Teacher had been brought back and was standing tied up on the portico with Pilate.

He stood quietly with His hands bound behind His back. Noah thought He didn't look much like a dangerous criminal. The three men stopped to watch.

They heard Pilate say, "Is this true that you're 'King of the Jews'?"

"Those are your words, not mine," Yeshua replied.

Pilate told the high priests and the accompanying crowd, "I find nothing wrong here. He seems harmless enough to me."[15]

Both Rocco and Luke breathed a sigh of relief. Noah began to hope this fiasco would end peacefully because this looked like a dangerous situation. The priests had already involved the governor, and that never ended well for the Jews. Something bad was happening, and no one seemed willing to stop it. His worse fears were realized as he saw how vehement the crowd had become. They were throwing rocks, rushing toward this mild-mannered man as if they would kill him themselves.

They shouted, "He's stirring up unrest among the people with his teaching, disturbing the peace everywhere, starting in Galilee and now all through Judea. He's a dangerous man, endangering the peace."

With that, Pilate realized that He was a Galilean and sent Him to Herod, who happened to be in Jerusalem at that time.[16]

The three men were unable to follow Him to Herod's court, but they stayed at a distance just to see what would happen. It wasn't long before they saw the Teacher, hands still tied, but someone had thrown a purple cloak on him and a crown of thorns on His head. Blood was staining his face making it difficult for him to see. The soldiers headed back to Pilate's palace, dragging Yeshua with them.

Luke still had hope things would work out. "See, they've put an expensive cloak on Him. Maybe they will let Him go." Then they noticed the "crown" had been shoved on His head and the blood was running down His face.

Noah still wrestled with what they had said about Him being a "dangerous man." He had seen the man over the last few years, and He was gentle with everyone. He had a small group of followers, but never had he seen a sword or any kind of weapon that might be used to overthrow the government. Everywhere He went, people were healed of illnesses, the blind and deaf were made whole. Nothing made sense to him right now.

Pilate seemed to have devised a new plan. "You brought this man to me as a disturber of the peace. I examined Him in front of all of you and found there was nothing to your charge. And neither did Herod, for he has sent Him back here. It's clear that He's done nothing wrong, let alone anything deserving death. I'm going to warn Him to watch His step and let Him go."

At that, the crowd went wild: "Kill him! Give us Barabbas!" (Barabbas had been thrown in prison for starting a riot in the city and for murder.)

Pilate still wanted to let Yeshua go, and so spoke out again. But they kept shouting back, "Crucify! Crucify Him!"

He tried a third time. "But for what crime? I've found nothing in Him deserving death. I'm going to warn Him to watch His step and let Him go."

But they kept at it, a shouting mob demanding that He be crucified. And finally, they shouted him down. Pilate caved in and gave them what they wanted. He released the man thrown in prison for rioting and murder and gave them Yeshua to do whatever they wanted.[17]

Luke and Rocco now realized the crowd was too riled up, and no one was going to stop the inevitable. Barabbas, that dangerous thief, was going to be released. When they heard Pilate give the order to have the man flogged, they were familiar with that type of punishment. Noah was tempted to leave because he knew what was coming. Reflexively, his back hurt from the stinging blows.

Soldiers gathered around the prisoner, each holding a whip with strips of metal attached. Each blow would cut into the skin and cause ripping and tearing of flesh.

Noah was well acquainted with the damage from one of these weapons. He cringed and drew away at the sight of them, but he could not turn away. Something made his eyes stay riveted as they stripped the Teacher to the waist and the first blow fell. The Teacher only grunted as blood began to flow down His back, over His shoulders, and down His arms.

Again and again, the blows came. Noah could not believe that Yeshua was still standing. He remembered how he had fainted after the third hit, yet this man was still standing as blow after blow rained down on his back. There was a small river of blood on the bricks at His feet; His face was unrecognizable. The soldiers only stopped when it was apparent there was no skin left on His back and they were too tired to continue. The Teacher continued to stand with the blood flowing. If anyone bothered to look, they would have noticed that His face glowed with victory, not defeat.

Someone appeared with a wooden cross and laid it across the Teacher's shoulders. He was so weak it was quickly apparent that He could not carry it, and a bystander was pressed into service. "Carry this cross to Golgotha. We will do it there," the soldiers growled.

Noah, Luke, and Rocco decided to follow the procession. It wasn't far, and the road was crowded with spectators. By the time they arrived, the Teacher and two other men were being nailed to their crosses. They could hear a "crunch" as the huge nails were hammered into place. The victims were wailing and screaming in pain, but the Teacher remained silent. Someone had placed a placard above His head that read, "King of the Jews."

Then the crosses were raised and dropped into holes. The two other men cried out in agony, but Yeshua never cried or cursed the Romans. The bleeding had stopped, but the Teacher, Yeshua, was still alive. They could hear Him talking but were not sure what He said. He seemed to be speaking first to someone at the foot of the cross, then to someone else. He spoke softly at times, then other times, He would shout. The men were tempted to get closer, but the crowd prevented any movement.

A small group of followers were huddled nearby helping to support a woman who could be His mother. With her were several other women, and a few men. Noah recognized some of them as men he had seen with the Teacher while they were up in Nazareth. As he watched, he saw tears and expressions of sadness and disbelief on their faces. They couldn't believe what was happening either.

Noah and his companions had heard of the horror of crucifixion, but neither of them had ever witnessed such an event. They were spellbound between horror and curiosity. Noah was amazed that women were still among the small group of followers and thought someone should take them home. This was no place for ladies. He kept hoping someone would show up and stop the soldiers from finishing their cruel task.

Hour after hour, they sat and watched. Still the Teacher did not cry out or curse. The hour for the noon meal went unnoticed as none of them could eat. Many of the crowd had left, growing tired of watching the gruesome scene. The small huddle of friends and family stayed, crying, and pleading with the Teacher to stop this madness. It was getting on toward mid afternoon, and the day had grown completely dark.

None of them could explain the darkness that settled so long. They could barely see the men on the crosses. There were no clouds to hide the sun, but it was as if the sun just stopped shining. Then the earth began to shake so violently the men had to hold onto nearby rocks to keep from being thrown to the ground. They continued to hear the Teacher talking to the crowd but were too far away to hear it all. Then when the chaos was becoming unbearable, they each heard a shout from the Teacher as He said, "It is finished." With that, He bowed His head and gave up His spirit.[18] It was clear that He was dead. The soldiers came and stuck their swords into His side, but He did not flinch. The other men were still alive, so the soldiers broke their legs so they could not hold themselves up by their feet. Obviously, they wanted this to be over as much as the onlookers.

The Healer

Luke, Rocco, and Noah stayed where they were with the anguish of the day written on their faces. Should they go home? Should they stay and help? The indecision kept them standing there, staring at each other in disbelief.

Later that evening before Passover was to begin, they saw a man known as Joseph come and claimed the Teacher's body and carried it off to a tomb nearby. The three men continued to follow along with the crowd but with no destination in mind. The soldiers weren't going to need healers today. He was dead. The volunteers hurriedly wrapped the man in cloths, put Him into the tomb, then waited while the soldiers placed a huge stone over the entrance.

Pilate had heard the rumor that the Teacher had said He would rise from the dead. As governor he had sent the soldiers to make sure the followers did not come and take the body away to claim He had risen. With these soldiers sitting in front of the tomb, nobody was getting into that tomb tonight. As night settled on them, the three men headed home to think about and discuss the events of the day. They did not know that the implications of this day would resonate through the ages to come.

Chapter 13

When the men arrived back in Bethany, they found Zeb in a state of agitation, pacing the floor alternating with sitting with his head in his hand. Word had reached him of the events of the day. He acknowledged Noah and his friends, but they could see that he had been crying.

"What is going to become of us? I was sure that He was the Messiah. Now the One we had such hope for is dead and all our plans for a savior are lost."

Luke took Zeb in his arms, and together they stood rocking and crying. "Brother, I don't understand it all yet, but I'm sure we will in time." Luke tried to comfort Zeb.

"Why did He let them do this to Him? He never did anything to hurt anyone, yet they had Him killed."

Zeb continued to sit with his head in his hands. The quiet in the room became heavy as each man was lost in his own thoughts. Noah wanted to take his father in his arms and tell him that everything was going to work out, but he knew that it wasn't. He wasn't quite sure why, but he knew that life would never be the same.

"My son, tell me again what you saw today." Zeb turned to Noah, and the look on his face told Noah that this was the most important question his father had ever asked him.

"I told you about them putting Him on the cross. He kept talking to those close by and sometimes He would shout. About noon, the sky went dark, and it was like nighttime. There were no clouds in the sky, but it seemed like the sun stopped shining for about three hours. We were all afraid. We later heard the crowds say that the temple curtain was torn that day from top to bottom. It must have been from the earthquake. We saw buildings shaking and we could hardly stand. Then toward mid afternoon I clearly heard Him say, 'It is finished.' I don't know what was finished, but then He died. The soldiers came and pierced His side, but He was already dead. I'm sure of it. The most amazing part was that He never cried or cursed the Roman guards. I felt like He was in control, not the soldiers."

Luke joined in. "First, they gave Him a terrible beating, then they took Him out to the Place of the Skull to crucify Him. But all that time, He never cursed the Romans."

When Noah and Luke had finished their narrative, Zeb sat quietly until he excused himself and went outside to walk and think. Luke and Rocco talked quietly about what they had seen and heard, neither of them had an explanation.

Noah was almost asleep when Zeb burst through the door. He seemed to have changed. His eyes were clear, his head held high, and his voice was strong.

"I've been thinking this through and talking to Jehovah. I'm beginning to understand some of this. Come, friends, sit down and listen. There must be an explanation for all this. I think it starts with the sacrifices." He laughed. "For thousands of years, the priests have been making sacrifices for us to cover our sins. Remember, this Teacher, Yeshua, claimed to be the Son of God. Now Jehovah has sent Him here to die, to bring us salvation. Because the curtain in the temple was torn, we can now go directly to God and confess our sins and receive forgiveness. That's why the curtain was torn. No person could have gone so high up to tear that curtain. It was from Jehovah. That curtain represented our sin that separated us from God. We won't need the priests anymore. What He finished was *our* salvation. It's all there in the holy scriptures if we had only paid closer attention. Remember He said He would rise from the dead. Well, I believe He will. If He said He would, then it will happen. The scriptures say that in three days, He will rise. So, if He doesn't, then I'm wrong and we have no hope. But if He does, then nothing can keep Him in the grave and we have hope for all time. We will have forgiveness. Remember the prophet Isaiah said:

> [4]"Surely he took up our pain
>   and bore our suffering,
>   yet we considered him punished by God,
>   stricken by him, and afflicted.
> [5]But he was pierced for our transgressions,
>   he was crushed for our iniquities;
>   the punishment that brought us peace was on him,
>   and by his wounds we are healed.
> [6]We all, like sheep, have gone astray,
>   each of us has turned to our own way;
>   and the Lord has laid on him
>   the iniquity of us all.
>
> [7]He was oppressed and afflicted,
>   yet he did not open his mouth;
>   he was led like a lamb to the slaughter,
>   and as a sheep before its shearers is silent,
>   so he did not open his mouth."[20]

Luke listened intently as hope began to blossom in him. As recognition came, he began to nod his head in agreement. "You are thinking clearly, brother. I should have remembered that too. But I got caught up in the horror of the day and forgot the teachings that I know so well. Forgive me, God, for my unbelief. Praise be to Jehovah who has brought us salvation this day."

"But how does His death bring us salvation?" Noah asked. That was the big question.

"Oh, my son. The holy writings tell us if we had only listened. The prophet Isaiah wrote:

> "Yet it was the Lord's will to crush him and cause him to suffer,
>   and though the Lord makes his life an offering for sin,

> he will see his offspring and prolong his days,
>   and the will of the Lord will prosper in his hand.
> [11]After he has suffered,
>   he will see the light of life and be satisfied;
>   by his knowledge my righteous servant will justify
>   many, and he will bear their iniquities."[21]

And again, King David wrote:

> "The Lord is my rock, my fortress and my deliverer my
>   God is my rock, in whom I take refuge, my shield
>   and the horn of my salvation, my stronghold"[22]

"How could we have forgotten that?" Zeb was crying and laughing at the same time. "In order to take our transgressions, He had to die. He could have stopped the execution, but don't you see, He was giving His life instead of us. He will come back, just like He said. Jehovah always keeps His promises."

Noah heard his father and wanted to believe him. 5here had to be some justification for the events of the day. Maybe if he proved this man could rise from the dead, he would be able to believe. He would wait to see if he could come out of that tomb before making his decision. 5hey could all get some sleep tonight, but Noah's hope depended on just one thing-an empty tomb.

Chapter 14

The morning dawned clear and warm. The city was quiet, with little commerce, due to the holiday. The two thieves were removed from their crosses and buried in a pauper's grave. The Teacher's followers seemed to have disappeared. Noah, Luke, and Rocco looked all over the city but were not surprised the men could not be found. After the events of this week, they had probably left the city.

By late afternoon, it was clear there would be no further business needed on the streets. Rocco returned to his family home, but Luke and Noah strolled the streets in friendly silence. They were about to buy some hot tea from a vendor, when Noah noticed a man staggering near the dark alley down the street. He thought he recognized the man from the day before but could not be sure. His clothes were dirty but well made. His face was a cloud of anguish and pain.

Noah walked toward him to see if he needed help. As he did so, he recognized the man as the Roman soldier who had stood right next to the cross of the Teacher. Gone was the swagger of his walk. Gone was the haughty stance he showed all day before. In their place was a broken man, trying to drown his pain in a sea of spirits.

"Can we help you, sir?" Noah asked politely.

"No, no one can help me now," he said as he staggered off.

It seemed clear this man had drunk too many spirits, so Noah and Luke brought him to a table and sat with him. For a long time, they said nothing. The man continued to sob, great raking wails that tore at their hearts as they tried to console him. When it seemed that he might be sobering up, they tried to find out what had happened to make him so distraught.

"Can you tell us what is going on with you?" Luke inquired. "It's all about what happened yesterday," he continued to sob. "Tell us what you remember."

"They made me do it. They made me kill an innocent man. I'm a good person, I take care of my family, I honor my government, and yet I killed an innocent man." He continued to sob.

"Can you tell us why you say He was innocent?" Noah asked cautiously.

"There was something different about Him. I've never seen anyone who could stand that many lashes and still walk. And then He never cried out on the cross, no cursing, no tears, no moans, nothing. There were no real charges against Him, yet it seemed everyone wanted Him dead. I can't understand why so many people wanted Him dead. He died so quickly too when there was no explanation for that either. And the darkness was impossible to explain. What happened to the sunshine? There were no clouds, but no light either! I can't help but think He controlled the day, not us."

"What did He say?" Noah asked.

"Well, He did ask someone named John to take care of His mother. Then He held a conversation with one of the thieves. He told the thief that he would see paradise with him that day. He was planning to be somewhere together with that man today, and then He said something I will never forget. He prayed for us, the ones executing Him. He said He forgave us. He FORGAVE US! I've never been forgiven for anything in my life. How could He forgive us? I just don't understand it." With that, his sobbing resumed.

Luke sat quietly through this narrative. He had never seen anyone in such anguish. His voice carried the weight of what he was about to say.

"That's what Jehovah God does. He forgives. This man was a very special person sent by God to make a way for us to know Him. Don't blame yourself. He could have come down from that cross at any time, but He stayed so we could know the Father. That's who He was talking to, so He could get through that ordeal. You need only ask for forgiveness; confess your sins and He will forgive."

Noah walked a distance away to think and consider what the man had said while Luke spoke further about the promised Messiah. Too much was happening too fast for Noah to understand all of it. So much depended on the grave and if it would be empty the next day. If the body was still there after three days, Yeshua could not be the promised Messiah. If the grave was empty, he was going to have to reconsider what he believed about this man. He was going to make sure that he saw all of it for himself.

As Noah looked back at Luke and the Roman soldier, they sat closely together with tears in both their eyes, talking softly as Luke reassured him again of forgiveness from Jehovah. Finally, the Roman stopped crying, bowed his head, and simply said, "I'm so sorry." That was all he could manage.

For two days, the city slept. The men could feel the city take a sigh of relief since their fears of an insurrection had been relieved. The Roman guards seemed confident that peace would be restored to the Jews after the execution of that rabble rouser. The priests had returned to the temple and Yeshua's followers had disappeared. There were rumors that a man had committed suicide outside the city and that he had been the one who led the guards to Yeshua. Not much notice was taken, since one more death didn't mean much after what had happened there.

On the third morning, Zeb insisted Noah and his friends go to the tomb where Yeshua was laid. He was sure the Messiah would not be there, but Noah was reluctant to be so near to the guards. It was never safe for a Jewish man to be too close, for fear of being arrested. Jewish men had disappeared all over Judea since the Romans took control. But Zeb would not waiver in his request.

"You must go for me. This may be the only time I've ever asked anything of you. I would go myself, but I'm just not able to do it. Go, and come back and tell me all you have seen."

With Luke and Rocco busy with their work, Noah agreed to go alone. He knew where the tomb was located, so he went before dawn to lessen the chances of meeting anyone on the way. As he drew closer, he saw some women ahead, carrying bundles in their arms. He heard them discussing who would roll away the big stone and he thought to offer his help, but he just wasn't sure he wanted to get involved. He wasn't sure he could move the stone anyway. He had agreed to this errand for his father, but he was not going to linger. This was a place for the dead, not for the living, he thought.

As they neared a garden near the tombs, Noah felt his heart hammering in his chest. What would he find there? He worried that the soldiers and the Teacher's followers would be in a big fight. Some had said the followers were going to steal the body, and he did not want to get into that fight. It would be a slaughter. The soldiers were armed with swords and shields, while His followers were known to be fishermen and common laborers. What hope did they have in a fight?

The quiet of the night still hung in the air as the women crept closer. He decided to hang back among the trees to see what would happen. As he got close enough to see the tomb, he was shocked that the guards were asleep, and the tombstone was rolled to one side. He saw the women rush in and immediately come back out. They were murmuring and excited about something they had experienced in the tomb. He heard them say the tomb was empty and wondered where the body could be. The women immediately rushed off, saying they had to tell the other followers.

Noah stayed where he was. Zeb had warned him that the tomb might be empty. He remembered that Zeb said that if the Teacher rose from the grave, they had hope at last. Could it be true?

He must go see for himself. So quietly and with great care not to make any noise, he made his way past the sleeping guards, to the mouth of the tomb. He peeked in and decided to go on inside since no one was around to catch him there. He looked around and saw the headscarf, carefully folded, and laid to one side, and the wrap they had used on the body. What could that mean? Surely, they wouldn't unwrap the body to take it away. And why were the guards still sleeping? Didn't they know the punishment for sleeping on the job was certain death?

He turned to go and spotted a woman who had stayed behind, weeping, in the garden. Maybe she would be able to clear up some of the mystery. He made his way to her, careful not to startle her in her grief.

"Excuse me, ma'am. Do you know anything about the Teacher who was buried here?" Noah asked.

"Oh, my dear child," she exclaimed. "I came to honor him in the tomb, but instead I found him alive. He was here and spoke to me. He's alive, he's alive! How can I cry at such a wonderful day?"

"Are you sure it was Him?" Noah asked.

"Oh, yes, I'm sure. My eyes were opened, and I saw Him. He spoke to me and called me by name. Son, you must believe because it is true."

Noah thought maybe he could learn more from the followers. Because this woman was hysterical. "I hear he had a group of followers. Do you think you could tell me where to find them?"

"I can take you to them. A small group is meeting together this morning. Follow me."

With that she turned and ran back through the garden, out into the streets of Jerusalem, through the marketplace, and down to a small dwelling that seemed out of place in this section of town. She climbed the stairs and knocked softly on the wooden door. It was opened almost immediately to a group of somber men who were gathered around a table for a meal.

"Mary, what do you want?" One man asked.

"He's alive. I saw Him and He's alive!" She sang out.

"What do you mean? We all saw Him dead and some of us even helped bury Him."

"I only know He is alive. He was dead and now He is alive," she responded. "Oh, happy day! He kept his promise!"

"I'm going to see for myself," one man said. "Wait, John, I'm going also," said another.

None of the men were aware of Noah standing there waiting to talk to them. He could only follow the small group that ran out of the room, down the stairs, and back through the garden. The one named John was running ahead of the others and raced right into the open tomb. By that time, Noah had heard their names and knew the other man was Simon, the one the Teacher called Peter. Noah was left standing, as the rest of the men gathered in the tomb trying to understand what had happened.

While he waited, Noah considered all he had seen the last three days—the horrible execution, the burial, the soldier, the encounter with the woman near the grave, and now, these followers. Some of the verses of holy scripture came to mind that had meant little when he memorized them for the priest, so many years ago. One kept running through his head:

> *Do not fear, for I have redeemed you.*
> *I have summoned you by name; you are mine.*
> *When you pass through the waters, I will be with you.*
>   *and when you pass through the rivers,*
>   *they will not sweep over you.*
> *When you walk through the fire, you will not be*
>   *burned the flames will not set you ablaze.*
> *For I am the Lord your God, the Holy One of Israel, your Savior.*[23]

He had often wondered how God would redeem Israel; this land promised to Israel so many years ago. So much time had passed, many had given up any hope for redemption. Now he wondered if this was the plan all along. To be redeemed meant to be bought with a great price. The idea of a conquering hero on a horse faded into a man on a donkey, dying on a cross. Someone who would be a Savior, a redeemer. Redemption through a death! He tucked that thought away until he could talk it over with Luke and his father.

The men came out of the tomb and started back to the house, forgetting that Noah was waiting. He needed to talk to them, but they were so busy talking about the empty tomb that he could only walk and listen.

"Don't you remember that He said He would rise again," the one called Peter stated. "I know I doubted as much as anyone. I even denied that I knew Him when He was being tried. How can I ever ask Him to forgive me?"

"Brother, He forgives." Another man consoled him. They must be brothers by the way they talked. "I know He will forgive you. He loves you so much. Wherever He is, I know He will find us, and when He does, we can ask Him all our questions. Let's go back and tell the others about this."

Noah felt like he had learned all he was going to get from these men today, so he turned for home. The followers of Yeshua did not even notice.

As he approached his home, he heard loud chattering from a house full of men and women. They were gesturing, laughing, and talking all at once. He saw his father and nodded for him to come outside.

"I have much to tell you," Noah said.

"Son, tell me everything. Don't leave anything out," Zeb declared.

Noah told him everything, from the empty tomb and the encounter with the woman, meeting the followers, hearing them talk about the Teacher, and finally, he began to tell his father of the remembered scriptures and the references to redemption.

Zeb did not interrupt until Noah became quiet. "This man was the Messiah. There is much to understand about the execution. We know that the Messiah could have stopped it all, but He did not. Why not, I ask you? He made

97

himself our sacrifice before His Father so that we could be called righteous. Right now, the main thing is to believe in Him and the resurrection from the dead. We all know that no person could ever do that—only Jehovah Himself. Now Yeshua has done so. He had to be God to do what He did. This will certainly not sit well with the Romans. We can expect trouble from them. "

There were so many more questions Noah wanted to ask, but it became more and more difficult to identify what they were. His father sat with him late into the night helping him understand the sacrifice needed before Jehovah and how a Messiah was the only person who could provide that. They spent a long time talking about redemption and why humans needed what only God could give.

As dawn approached, Noah could not object anymore. The tears of sorrow and regret welled in his eyes and his heart melted in him. He saw himself as Jehovah must see him and he was ashamed. Acknowledging that he needed a Redeemer was a big step for him, this independent, strong young man he had worked hard to become. Yet he could not deny the reality of that empty tomb. It was empty and there was no body. Yeshua had risen from the dead and deserved his undivided loyalty. Papa was right all along. He hung his head and began talking to the God he had come to believe could hear him.

"God, I know you must be there. If you heard Joseph in slavery, Daniel in the lion's den, or Moses at the Red Sea, you must be able to hear me too. I know I've been sinful and need to be forgiven just as much as that Roman soldier. I've carried anger and pain from my treatment by Enoch and from the thieves on the road. They tried to ask my forgiveness, but I was stubborn and would not forgive. Please forgive me and use me as your servant for the rest of my life."

"Thank you, Lord Almighty, God of the Universe," Zeb prayed as he grabbed Noah and hugged him, saying, "I have prayed for you since you were a boy. I love the man you have become. Continue on the road with our Savior and you will never be alone."

They sat in silence as the sun rose. The day passed in calm on the little farm outside of Jerusalem, but they had no idea of the storm brewing in the city.

PART III

Persecution

Chapter 15

The weeks that followed were filled with unrest. Pilate was determined to find the body of Yeshua to prove He had not risen from the dead. Soldiers were dispersed to every corner of Jerusalem to find the followers and force them to reveal the whereabouts of the body. They even dug up graves of recently departed criminals in hopes of finding the Teacher.

With all the threats, the followers tried to stay hidden until it got too dangerous, they disappeared. Some said they had gone up to Galilee. Others thought they had dispersed, never to be heard from again.

Luke, Rocco, and Noah stayed at his parents' house for several more weeks. Rumors began to circulate among Zeb's friends that Yeshua had been seen in the flesh. Luke listened to these stories with growing interest.

As Luke and Noah were sitting in the courtyard three weeks after the execution, Luke began to speak about their future.

"I've been thinking about all that has happened here, and I believe God is telling me that someone must write this down. The next generations of people will need to know what has happened here. I'm thinking about trying to find His followers and talk to them about that idea. What do you think?"

"I think it will be a monumental task," Noah responded. "I too would like to find His followers to just hear more about His time with them."

"We could start with some of Zeb's friends. They might have an idea about where to look."

"Then I think we should talk it over with your parents and Rocco and make a plan."

"I'm in!" Noah exclaimed. "I want to know more also. When I remember what we saw of Him, many things have started to make sense to me."

That night after the dinner meal, Luke called Zeb, Sarah, Miriam, and Rocco together.

"Noah and I have an idea that we want to discuss. I want to talk to the followers of Yeshua, the only ones who can help me write their story. God is telling me that this is too important not to tell coming generations. What do you think?"

Zeb was the first to speak. "I agree with the idea, but I hate to lose Noah so soon after he got here. For many years we did not know if he was alive or dead. Now he is not only alive, but a follower too. But I know how important this is and I agree. I remember that the messengers said at His birth that this was news for all people. That includes those who will come after us."

Sarah nodded in agreement and leaned over to give Noah a hug.

Zeb spoke up. "You must go. If the Almighty is calling, who are we to say you should not go?"

Miriam surprised everyone when she spoke up. "I think you should go, but I'm going with you. I am strong and able to help. I want to follow Him also and you might need a woman along the way. I would also like to know more about your healing ministry, which you can show me while we walk."

Sarah looked doubtfully at Miriam. "The travel to Galilee will be difficult. Are you sure you want to try this?"

"I'm sure, Mother."

"I won't try to stop you. Jehovah God go with you." Sarah leaned over and took Miriam in her arms and wept.

All agreed with nods, smiles, and hugs for a safe journey.

"It's settled then," Luke said. "We will leave in two days. We have much to prepare."

Two days later, the small group was ready to embark on the journey toward Galilee, where the followers were said to be. It would take two or three days to get there, but the men did not know if they would find him in Galilee or need to continue searching so they prepared for much longer. Each person carried a pack with a sleeping blanket, a jar for water, a sack for food, and a walking stick, so important on these rocky, rutted roads they would follow.

As they started out early that day, Noah was concerned that Miriam would not be able to keep up with the men, but he was soon surprised by her vitality and endurance. She was often at the head of the group, leading the way. It was a pleasant day with bright sunshine and a cool breeze.

They soon discovered that Rocco could sing, and Miriam joined in. Their voices blended making sweet music to walk and talk. Together they made the journey seem like a short stroll.

At the end of the day, they had not seen any of the followers. But they rested well and began again the next day.

For two more days they continued north toward Galilee. Several times they were joined by travelers, and each time, Luke would engage them in conversation about the events in Jerusalem. From them, they gleaned bits and pieces of information about the Teacher, who had traveled these roads often and would stop to heal the sick, the blind, and the lame.

There was one story that He stopped in Samaria and talked with a woman at Jacob's well. Yes, they were sure it was in Samaria, where no Jew would consider conversing with a woman. That stop resulted in the whole town coming to believe on Him as the Messiah.

They were encouraged by these reports and continued. They too went through Samaria and on to Galilee. When they arrived at Nazareth, they stopped at a place where He had made His home. They had to ask several people how to find it, but Nazareth was small, and they found it easily enough.

There they met Mary, Yeshua's mother, and His brothers James and Titus. Mary began telling them stories about Yeshua as a child. Her face became radiant when she spoke His name. She even spoke openly of the execution, how difficult it had been, but expressed such hope and joy to know that He was alive. The pain of the crucifixion had dimmed as the reality of His resurrection took hold in her.

Luke informed her of their mission, and she agreed to help. She suggested that they go to the sea, since He had spent such wonderful times there with His followers.

When they left the next morning, James and Titus joined them. It was less than a day's journey to the sea, so they were able to get there as the sun was setting. They made an evening meal and sat around a fire to discuss their strategy to find the followers.

Luke thought they should wait. "I think if we stay here, they will find us."

"We need to spread out and look," Rocco said impatiently. He was ready to go looking immediately.

James was more thoughtful. "I did not believe Him when, as a child, He told us that He was from heaven. I thought He was speaking as one of us kids. Now I know He was serious. I should have listened more carefully. I can't believe that I grew up in the same house and did not believe Him."

Luke looked at James and Titus with love in his eyes and said, "James, you will have many valuable lessons to teach us all. The most important thing is what we do now. If you focus on what you ignored as a child, you will miss the lessons He came to teach us."

"Brother don't blame yourself. Blame isn't going to help us now. I did not believe Him either," replied Titus. "I am sorry also, but I can't let that keep me from serving Him now."

"Let's put aside our plans until tomorrow when we are rested," Luke suggested.

They spread out on the sandy seashore and listened to the sounds of the sea, the birds cawing, the waves sloshing, the creaking of moored boats. Such a peaceful place, it was not a surprise to find out Yeshua had come here to rest and teach His followers.

The next morning, Miriam was the first to awaken and begin the meal. She woke the others and said, "Breakfast is ready. I think you need to come check on some men who have gathered in the distance. They might know the Teacher and His followers. Come, let's find out."

After breakfast, Luke and Noah were the first to head toward the group gathered a short distance away. As they approached, Noah recognized the men who had rushed to the tomb ahead of him. He nudged Luke. "It's them. I recognize the men. You were right, they have found us."

The men looked up and greeted them warmly, "Come, friends, have some fish." "We have eaten, thank you," Luke replied.

Then Noah looked intently at the men. Not only did he recognize the two men, Peter, and John, he had seen at the empty tomb, but also the man he had seen on the cross. Could it be the same one?

He had heard from the woman at the tomb that He was risen, but this was different. He was seeing the Teacher for himself. He was spellbound by the sight of this man. He was the same man but different somehow. He had a glow about his face that was hard to describe. He was not a big man and there was nothing special about His appearance. He had brown hair that hung to His shoulders, dark skin, white teeth, and a warm smile. Noah looked closer and noticed the scars on his hands where the soldiers had nailed him to the cross.

As Noah looked, the man's eyes were sharp as knives, piercing his thoughts and intentions. The Teacher caught his eye and held them, as if with a magnet. Noah thought the Man was seeing into his very soul.

"Come join us," he said simply.

The men must have had astonished expressions on their faces as if they were seeing a ghost. Noah and Luke sat in the sand. By this time, Titus, James, Rocco, and Miriam had arrived. The Teacher just continued with His discussion as if the strangers were not there.

He said to them, "Why are you troubled, and why do doubts rise in your minds? Look at my hands and my feet. It is I! Touch me and see; a ghost does not have flesh and bones, as you see I have."

When He had said this, He showed them His hands and feet. And while they still did not believe it because of joy and amazement, He asked them, "Do you have anything here to eat?"

They gave Him a piece of broiled fish, and He took it and ate it in their presence.

He said to them, "This is what I told you while I was still with you: Everything must be fulfilled that is written about me in the Law of Moses, the Prophets, and the Psalms."

Then He seemed to open their minds so they could understand the scriptures. He told them, "This is what is written: The Messiah will suffer and rise from the dead on the third day, and repentance for the forgiveness of sins will be preached in his name to all nations, beginning at Jerusalem. You are witnesses of these things. I am going to send you what my Father has promised; but stay in the city until you have been clothed with power from on high."[24]

After He said this, the men began asking questions among themselves and it wasn't until things got quiet that they realized that the Teacher was no longer there.

The Healer

"Where has He gone?" Luke asked Simon, the one they now called Peter.

"He has left us. He has opened the holy scriptures to us so that we now understand much more than we did before. He says he isn't going to be with us much longer. But we are to go back home and wait for the power to come."

With that, they began to gather their belongings and leave. Luke and their entourage headed back to their camp to do the same. As they prepared to leave, they talked of the things they needed to discuss with the followers, but that could wait. They needed to get back to Jerusalem.

The journey home was quiet but purposeful. All were thinking of the future and what the resurrection meant for them. When they arrived back in Jerusalem, the city was in turmoil. Roman soldiers roamed the streets looking for anyone who might have information about the whereabouts of Yeshua's body. Anyone who could be identified as a follower was detained and questioned.

So much time had passed, they were becoming worried that the body would never been found. Several different rumors were being circulated; one was that the followers had come and stolen the body while the soldiers were sleeping. Another said that He had never died but had been revived while in the grave and then He had opened the tomb Himself. All the rumors were too easily refuted for anyone to take seriously, so the Romans continued to search.

Noah and Luke kept to their home in Bethany to avoid the soldiers. Luke continued to talk about writing the good news story, but there were many obstacles. He had not been with Jesus during His time on earth, so he would need lots of time with His followers. For background, he would need to go back to see Mary to talk about His days growing up in Nazareth.

When Zeb arrived home, he wanted to hear all the details of their adventures in Galilee. Noah tried to remember every detail, especially the experience of meeting the Teacher Himself. Zeb's eyes never strayed from him as he told of how the Man looked straight at him, knowing everything about him but saying nothing. He told of what the followers said about His stay with them and how He would not be here long.

"Where is He going?" Asked Zeb.

"That's not clear yet," Noah replied. "The followers said that He had to leave them to send power to them. They expect that to happen in a few days. There is a lot I don't know yet, but I think these men will help me learn more."

The following week, Luke, along with Titus and James, left to go to the city to find Peter and the rest of the followers. Noah stayed home to consider what to do next.

Noah worried about Daniel and William. Both men had been good friends to him at the farm and not only friends but had saved his life at the hands of Enoch. William would be so happy to hear the good news story. He had trusted Jehovah for the many years of his life. Now the fulfillment of his hope could be revealed. Noah was anxious to tell him that the Messiah had come and paid the ultimate sacrifice for mankind. He couldn't wait to tell him about the empty tomb that proved the Yeshua was who He said He was.

Daniel was another problem. He did not know the holy scriptures, had never gone to temple school, and did not know the laws of Moses. Convincing him of this good news was going to be a challenge.

"Jehovah, help me know what to do," he prayed.

When Luke returned, he was anxious to tell them of what he had seen and heard from the followers. Yeshua had left them, as He had said. Before He left, He gave them a charge.

"All authority in heaven and on earth has been given to me. Therefore, go and make disciples of all nations, baptizing them in the name of the Father and of the Son and of the Holy Spirit, and teaching them to obey everything I have commanded you. And surely, I am with you always, to the very end of the age."[25]

Luke was even more committed to writing the gospel story for coming generations. Peter had agreed to assist him, along with some other followers. In his excitement, he confessed that he would be leaving them soon. He trusted Noah to continue his healing ministry but his calling from Jehovah could not be ignored.

The followers were gathering in Jerusalem for the Feast of Pentecost and afterward were planning a strategy to spread the good news about the Christ. Luke couldn't describe this strategy yet, but Peter was planning to head north toward Samaria. Luke would be going with him. They had no idea that their experience at the Feast of Pentecost would change everything.

Epilogue

Noah did go back to the farm to see William and Daniel. As expected, William was overjoyed to hear all about the Christ who had defeated death. He also saw the amazing changes that had taken place in Noah's life. He now walked with confidence and strength. He talked freely about his newfound faith in his God, the horror of the crucifixion, the joy of the resurrection, and the charge to tell everyone on the earth.

Daniel was at first reluctant to accept this amazing story. He could not explain the change in Noah, but he was determined to find out what had changed Noah into this confident, warm, outgoing personality. As Noah gently told him of the importance of what had happened, he started to ask more questions.

Each time, Noah would share the story of Jesus and what the resurrection meant to him. He admitted that he could not believe until he saw the empty tomb. That meant that the man who had walked on the same roads as he, could also defeat death. No one before or since could do that. Even at that moment, men were dying in Jerusalem for the crime of loving Him as the Christ. Accepting Jesus as Messiah and Christ was not going to be an easy road. There would be dangers from the government, taunts from friends, and sometimes, even families would not believe. But he could not deny the empty tomb. It made all the difference. He saw the change in Noah and wanted the same for himself. After a time of questioning, he too felt compelled to believe.

What happened to the followers of Jesus? Did they disperse never to be seen or heard from again? Pentecost did change everything and everyone there. The Power came in a spectacular way. These humble fishermen had the Power to tell the world about the Savior who had risen from the dead and the strength to withstand the persecution to come. And it did come, driving them out of their homes, sending some to prison and many to their death.

Of the remaining eleven, all except John were martyred, but not before they told their story to the world. They died because they would not and could not deny the Teacher who rose from the dead. John was exiled on the Island of Patmos where he was able to write the final book of the Bible, Revelation.

The new followers of the Christ had a few years of peace and growth until Nero came to power about thirty years later. He began a systematic persecution that drove them out of the area, scattering as far as Asia and Europe taking the gospel story with them. They refused to deny the One who gives life, hope, and peace.

Jesus had said, *"I am the way and the truth and the life. No one comes to the Father except through me. If you really know me, you will know my Father as well. From now on, you do know him and have seen him."*[26]

The new believers took that seriously. Many died for that belief. Down through the ages, people continue to die for that same belief. It is not a popular belief now nor had it ever been popular. But it is still truth.

Endnotes

1. The New International Version Bible (2011), (Is. 61:1), Grand Rapids, Mi., Zondervan.
2. The New International Version Bible (2011), (Is. 61:1–3) Grand Rapids, Mi., Zondervan.
3. The New International Version Bible (2011), (Luke 2:14) Grand Rapids, Mi., Zondervan.
4. Holy Bible, New Living translation (Micah 5:2), Coral Stream, Ill., Tyndale House.
5. The New International Version Bible (2011), (Ps. 23:1–4), Grand Rapids, Mi., Zondervan.
6. The New International Version Bible (2011), (Ps. 103: 2–3), Grand Rapids, Mi., Zondervan.
7. Peterson, E. H. (2005), The Message: The Bible in Contemporary Language (Matt. 3:15), Colorado Springs, Co., NavPress.
8. Peterson, E. H. (2005), The Message: The Bible in Contemporary Language (Matt. 3:17), Colorado Springs, Co., NavPress.
9. Peterson, E. H. (2005), The Message: The Bible in Contemporary Language (Is. 7:14), Colorado Springs, Co., NavPress.
10. Peterson, E. H. (2005), The Message: The Bible in Contemporary Language (Isaiah 9:6-7), Colorado Springs, Co., NavPress.
11. Peterson, E. H. (2005), The Message: The Bible in Contemporary Language (Luke 4:17–19), Colorado Springs, Co., NavPress.
12. Peterson, E. H. (2005), The Message: The Bible in Contemporary Language (Luke 4:21), Colorado Springs, Co., NavPress.
13. The New International Version Bible (2011), (Luke 19:38–40), Grand Rapids, Mi., Zondervan.
14. Peterson, E. H. (2005), The Message: The Bible in Contemporary Language (Matt. 3:17), Colorado Springs, Co., NavPress.

15. Peterson, E. H. (2005), The Message: The Bible in Contemporary Language (Luke 23:3–4), Colorado Springs, Co., NavPress.
16. Peterson, E. H. (2005), The Message: The Bible in Contemporary Language (Luke 23:5), Colorado Springs, Co., NavPress.
17. Peterson, E. H. (2005), The Message: The Bible in Contemporary Language (Luke 23:14–15), Colorado Springs, Co., NavPress.
18. The New International Version Bible (2011), (John 19:30), Grand Rapids, Mi., Zondervan.
19. The New International Version Bible (2011), (Is. 52:7), Grand Rapids, Mi., Zondervan.
20. The New International Version Bible (2011), (Is. Isaiah 53;4-7), Grand Rapids, Mi., Zondervan.
21. The New International Version Bible (2011), (Is. 53:10–11), Grand Rapids, Mi., Zondervan.
22. The New International Version Bible (2011), (Ps. 18:2), Grand Rapids, Mi., Zondervan.
23. The New International Version Bible (2011), (Is 43: 1–3), Grand Rapids, Mi., Zondervan.
24. The New International Version Bible (2011), (Luke 24:37–49), Grand Rapids, Mi., Zondervan.
25. The New International Version Bible (2011), (Matt. 28:19–20), Grand Rapids, Mi., Zondervan.
26. The New International Version Bible (2011), (John 14:6–7), Grand Rapids, Mi., Zondervan.

Linda McClung graduated from Virginia Baptist Hospital School of Nursing, The College of New Jersey, and Seton Hall University. She spent fifty years as a nurse then retired to South Carolina to enjoy lakeside living near her family. After several serious health issues, she decided to write something for her grandchildren so that for years to come they would never forget what was important to her. She enjoys reading, gardening, and fishing in the lake. She lives in South Carolina with her husband, Ron.

www.ingramcontent.com/pod-product-compliance
Lightning Source LLC
LaVergne TN
LVHW091557060526
838200LV00036B/874